Cult of the De

Prologue

Father Ricci picked up the file note.
They were still active. He felt it.

STAFF – EYES - ONLY

Office of Community
Exorcism – Naples

File Note/Ricci
The Cult of the Dead - Naples
Full Title: The Church of Santa Maria
  delle Anime del le Purgatorio ad Arco

Thrived in Naples ONLY – 1401 to 1500 CE
Re-emerged in 1638, so continued to meet in secret.

Rituals. Buried dead monks twice. After the first

burial – when the flesh had decomposed, body and skulls were separated and placed into separate Ossuary's.

Believed the dead could make pleas on behalf of the living for a reduction of time In Purgatory.

Did Nostradamus take up with the cult in 1534 when his wife and child died from plague? He was known to have turned his back on religion and medicine. There are similarities between Nostradamus' prophecies published in Italy in 1550, and earlier verses linked to the cult.

Finally Disassociated by the RC Church in 1969.

Cult of the Dead

by
Thorne Hex

Copyright © Thorne Hex

The right to be identified as author has been asserted by the author in accordance with the Copyright, Designs and Patents Act 1988.

All rights reserved. No part of this publication may be reproduced, stored in a retrieval system, or transmitted in any form or by means, electronic, mechanical, photocopying, recording, or otherwise, without the prior permission of the author.

A CIP catalogue record for this title is available from the British Library.

All characters in this publication are fictitious, any resemblance to any real persons, living or dead, is purely coincidental.

ISBN –

Chapter 1
To Protect and Shield

Father Ricci unlocked the building and looked at her.

Michela De Luca was exhausted.

She paused as he held open the door to the old warehouse - as if she was having second thoughts.

'It's okay. You've been through a lot and I want to help. And who else is there?' he said.

The anxiety lines relaxed on her face, and she stepped carefully over the wooden threshold. The possibility of avoiding more sleepless nights and more vile dreams encouraged her forward.

The inner space was as functional as it was spartan. High beams bridged the gap beneath the huge ceiling and an intimidating but precise pentagram and circle took up most of the floor space. Michela had seen these things before and was holding back the bad recollections hinged to the experience.

Father Davide Ricci looked at her sternly.

'This may get rough,' he warned her.

She took a determined breath. 'What choice is there?' Michela asked and stepped into the Pentagram without waiting.

He gestured that she should sit, for her own safety. Her eyes followed as he walked the outer perimeter of the circle, sprinkling holy water and offering prayers of protection at each of the cardinal points.

'Close your eyes,' he commanded firmly. 'Don't open them unless I tell you…and pray the Hail Mary.' He reached into his robe pocket with his left hand and took out a set of wooden Rosary Beads that he lay across her palm.

'Hail Mary. Mother of God. Blessed art thou amongst women…' she began, counting a bead off between her thumb and forefinger, each time.

Father Davide stepped into the circle and made the sign of the cross on her forehead. He began to recite the verses of the Exorcism rite.

Michela cried out and convulsed. Her eyes glazed over, and she slipped out of consciousness. Suddenly, it was no longer Michela held fast in the circle.

'Fuck you,' rasped the demon. 'Fuck you Priest!' It hissed the word "priest" with such clarity and venom, Davide knew at once that this would not be a "gentle cleansing".

'Hasten to our call for help and snatch from ruination and from the clutches of the noonday evil this human being made in your image and likeness.' The Priest continued. There was no stopping here or the beast might permanently take ownership of her.

'I command you, unclean spirit, whoever you are, along with all your minions now attacking this servant of God, by the mysteries of the incarnation, passion, resurrection and the ascension of the Lord Jesus Christ, by the descent of the Holy Spirit, by the coming of the Lord for judgement, that you tell me by some sign your name, and the day and hour of your departure.'

Cult of the Dead

The demon slabbered, coughed and spat a thick globule of phlegm at the Priest, then laughed. It was a haunting laugh, that hung and lodged in the mind. 'Is that all you got, Priest?' It scorned. 'I think I might play with her. Pretty 'aint she? Don't tell me you didn't think about what you'd like to do to her.'

'I command you, moreover, to obey me to the letter.'

'Admit it Priest. You want to do things to her, don't you?'

'I who am a minister of God, despite my unworthiness; nor shall you be emboldened to harm in any way this creature of God, or the bystanders, or any of their possessions.' He continued, unshaken.

'You want to be like me, don't you, Priest? Stuck inside her?' It taunted.

It was a strong one. Usually, they began to fall silent at this point, as they fought fiercely to keep control of the victim. He placed a hand on Michela's forehead and offered a blessing of protection. The foul beast squirmed its head awkwardly, trying to shift its head from under his grip.

'Depart you Devil,' he commanded.

He laid the end of his ceremonial stole across the demon's head. 'See the cross of the Lord. Begone hostile power.'

The demon tried to wriggle free from under the stole, but Davide placed his right hand down firmly trapping it fast on its head.

'I cast you out unclean spirit, along with every Satanic power of the enemy...' 'Begone, then, in the name of the Father, the Son and the Holy

Spirit.' He made the sign of the cross in front of the demon with his right hand.

The entity fell silent, and Michela slumped forward.

He caught her and lifted her up gently and set her down, outstretched, on the chaise lounge to one side of the room. He covered her carefully with a warm blanket and placed a crucifix on the centre of her chest. Then he slipped a pillow under her head, gently, and knelt to pray.

It wasn't unusual that Michela slept for four hours. It was unusual, but not completely unknown to him, that when he awakened her, it was again the demon that spoke.

'We're not done, yet, Priest,' it challenged, slapping away the cup of tea he offered so that it smashed on the floor.

With that, it was gone. It left her. He felt its foul and heavy presence lift.

Michela's body fell back onto the pillow, and she slid immediately into an exhausted sleep.

Father Davide let her rest. He tried another cup of tea two hours later. He was concerned that she might have loved ones or family who might be anxious about where she was. Very few of his clients shared the true purpose of their visits with family or friends.

'How do you feel?' he asked.

'Better.. but so tired.' She sipped gratefully at her tea.

'I won't keep you long just now, but there are a couple of things I'd like to check.'

Michela nodded her ready agreement.

'When they invoked the Spirit, did they use a name to call it?'

'Squail,' she said, confidently. 'It's the last bit I remember.'

He nodded. 'And what was the name of the cult, again?'

'The Cult of the Summoned.'

'Not the Cult of the Dead?' He asked.

'No. I never heard it called that,' she told him.

He smiled. 'You must go home and get some rest. I'll get you a taxi.'

'No. It's okay. Thank you. I'll walk. I'm not far away.'

'I insist.' He picked up the phone, with the caring manner of a doctor, and dialled.

He let her finish her tea and then helped her into the cab. 'Call me, when you are rested,' he told her. 'Hopefully, that will be the end of it and you'll be able to sleep well again.'

'Thank you, Father. But…' She hesitated, 'I feel like there's something you are not telling me…'

'Nothing you need concern yourself with, just now, he assured her. 'Call me when you are properly rested and we'll meet and talk, or before, if you need to.'

Michela relaxed again. She wanted to know she could come back for more help, if needed.

Father Ricci went back into the warehouse, and sat at his desk, deep in thought.

He took out a piece of parchment from the top drawer and studied the content carefully.

'When the Rabbi shelves his tallit, and pacts, at once, with Christ to pray, an exiled Priest be summoned to it, and dark forces muster to evil play.'

'When demons numbered four assemble, over membrane void betwixt the realms, when four servants are taken to resemble, demons rise to gather souls.'

'And darkness draws on power abundant, taking weak and weakened souls, mantle force of good made spent, crossing freely to evil hold.'

'Pestilent curses eternal reign, baked, hot earth scorched to tinder dry, amidst turbulent floods that deign, the lower realms to make the same.'

He flicked the parchment over. It looked and felt genuine, but he had to be sure. Taking out his mobile he tapped in a number. Time to call in a favour.

The number was engaged and so he fired off a text message before dropping his mobile back in his pocket.

Chapter 2
The Cult of the Dead

How very 'Nostradamus,' Father Ricci thought, looking the verses over once more.

Outside of Rome, Naples was the only approved but low-key Centre of Exorcism. He found that especially perplexing as the city had a long history of being on the religious fringes, and the frequency of "spiritual concerns" in Naples, had risen way beyond the numbers reported for Rome.

Yet Rome had three permanent staff, and here in Naples, it was just himself.

The Cult of the Dead was not a secret.

Even today, in 2023, the council encouraged tourists looking for a real taste of the city's unique culture to visit the Fontanelle Cemetery, the Church of Santa Maria delle Anime del Purgatorio ad Arco, and the Catacombs of San Gennaro - between them boasting an array of monks' skulls, and headless bodies. All seemed connected to the cult.

Otherwise known as the Cult of the Dead, it was always unique and exclusive to Naples.

He could see how having the dead speak on your behalf to avoid or reduce the time you might have to spend in Purgatory would appeal to a mostly illiterate and poor population who almost certainly couldn't then afford to pay for the

Catholic Church's Indulgences for the same benefits.

The cult last re-emerged in 1638.

The Church didn't disassociate from them until 1969, so clearly they had always been there.

'Why so late'? He wondered.

'Did the Church suddenly become aware of other reasons? Other activities?'

From merely 'speaking with the dead' is it an inevitable progression to want to try to 'raise them?' he wondered.

He suspected human nature dictated it might be, for some.

Chapter 3
Summoned

The phone call from Cardinal Tolcini broke Davide's thoughts, and demanded his immediate presence at the Vatican. The senior priest rarely missed an opportunity to remind him 'Priests don't get to work from 9am to 5am,' and he didn't disappoint on this occasion.

Davide rang for a taxi to take him to the station in Naples. Rail Italia provided up to fifty-six departures a day and the high-speed journey could take as little as 1 hour and 12 minutes.

Before setting out for Rome he photographed the ancient verses with his mobile, wrapped the document in a secure binding, and then addressed the envelope to a Marilyn Forster at the British Library. If anyone could get the document examined and authenticated, it was her.

Marilyn and he had been firm friends since they met in Knossos when they were both researching the beliefs of the Cult of the Bull, thirty years before.

He locked up the warehouse and checked it was secure. The Vatican would rather not have the nature of his work waved in front of the scoop-hungry press, which was why the preferred location was in a side street in Naples near to an industrial part of the city

He posted the document at the station. The Vatican wasn't having this one! It wasn't so much that they hid or censored documents – except for a few. They just disappeared into the well-oiled and sizeable archives, but nobody actually had the job of sending back a location number once they were stored. Formal requests to recover a document were incredibly slow, which was not about any wilful 'resistance' so much as not having enough staff to cope with such a huge resource.

The faster train left 19.30 hours and he was boarding another taxi in Rome just an hour and a half later.

Cardinal Tolcini greeted him warmly but his face gave nothing away. It never did.

'We're sending you to England.' He announced.

'What? Why? And who will continue my work here, Father?'

'Ah! Well! Your work can wait.' Cardinal Tolcini smiled at him. 'Rome wasn't built in a day you know.'

'But Your Eminence, we've had a huge increase in the number of demonic possessions. People need our help...and we both know the history of Naples...it's much worse than Rome...and yet Rome is much better supported?' He protested.

'You're not still banging on about that cult stuff are you, Davide? We've been through all that...'

'And if I can produce more evidence?'

'Do you have it with you?'

'No...but...'

'Then it will just have to wait,' snapped Tolcini. 'There are never enough hours and never enough of us,' he insisted. I need you to go to England, tomorrow.'

The way he added tomorrow made Davide think that he'd just decided the timing was an essential part of the duties.

'What's so urgent?'

'We've had a Rabbi who has thrown in his 'tallit,' so to speak. He's marrying a good Catholic girl, and I'm sure in time he will become a great asset to our Holy Order. But you know what they're like 'upstairs' – 'all smoke and mystery.'

Tolcini laughed at his own little quip aimed at the most senior council. 'They need someone to check him out quickly. They agree with me - we may well be in need of him to represent us on the Inter-Faith front.'

'And if there are complications here?'

'Don't worry about that for now. We'll take care of it - if its urgent.'

'And if I say 'no'?

Cardinal Tolcini was not a man who liked to be challenged directly.

'That's not the response I expected, Father.'

'I have a condition.' Davide ventured.

'Well…this is highly irregular.'

'Or I resign,' said Davide.

An awkward silence dropped between them.

Davide knew he was pushing the boundaries well beyond what was expected, but he didn't doubt also that there would be a holy host of questions to be answered if he did resign.

'Name your condition,' said Tolcini, after a moment.

'If Michela De Luca, or any of my other clients develop complications, I want the Vatican to fly them over to where I am, or get me back here quickly' said Davide, flatly.

'Very well.' Said Tolcini. 'But don't forget you'll be looking for my support to hold the Naples project open when you get back. I shall have to reflect on quite how I feel about that.'

Davide nodded his assent, and gave a respectful nod to his superior. He felt he'd pushed it as far as he could, and the old sage had a point. He'd need his help when he got back – with or without evidence.

'Shelving the tallit!' Now why was that somehow, familiar?

He made his way to the central office to pick up his ticket details, and to book a Vatican room for the night.

Chapter 4
Rabbi Saul Joachim

The date was agreed and Saul could see no other way forward. He settled up as much 'community business' as he could - so far as he could - and then announced his intended resignation in the notices following the service.

People were upset. So was he, actually. He'd been the Rabbi of the Menorah Synagogue for five years and he felt he'd made a real difference.

His fiancée, however, was Catholic with a very large 'C.' Not only were her parents very wealthy, they were lifelong supporters and beneficiaries to the church.

It was absolutely clear from the first conversation with Francis James, her father, that the hand of his daughter Sasha was irrevocably contingent on any future family being raised in the one, true Christian faith.

In all other respects, the union between the Rabbi and Sasha met with every approval, but the matter of future faith, it seemed, was entirely non-negotiable.

He'd held out for as long as he could. Sasha had even suggested 'running away' to Israel with him in order that they might develop their relationship fully without such interference. A sense of obligation to family, and his work as a Rabbi, meant he knew the value of family support – especially if the family was very well placed, and able and willing to help them to get established.

Of course, it was reassuring and good for their 'trust' that Sasha was committed enough to give it all up for him.

His decision to *'shelve the tallit'* was therefore his own and hadn't come easily to him. Far from it. But he could see that it was the only decision that would not create a lasting 'rift' with Sasha's family, and ultimately, he felt his future place and happiness was most definitely with her.

He couldn't begin to imagine a future without her, and it was the great strength and the practicalities of his faith that gave him the resolve to put her more pressing need for the Christian version of the sanctity of marriage ahead of his own callings.

The idea of a straight transfer into the Catholic faith was made plausible by the extensive influence Francis seemed to hold as a beneficiary, and it was obvious to all that there were similarities in the duties of service to the community required by both faiths - although he suspected privately he might come to resent any noticeable loss of autonomy, arising from the changes.

It had the added benefit that it would smooth the way into the James' family, and, in truth, Saul wasn't quite sure if it was Francis or Mary James who was the real driving force.

Francis had the means, there was no doubt about that. But the way Mary had 'sung from the same hymn sheet' with a fuller understanding and justification than that shown by Francis that evinced him it was 'mother-in-law' to be, Mary, who was 'wearing the trousers' in the matter.

One of the many blessings of working a faith is that it teaches you when to hold your private thoughts in check, while looking ahead to the end game.

With a fair wind, and by focussing his skills in an Inter-Faith capacity, it was entirely possible that he'd end up working alongside Jewish communities – albeit with a different 'brand name' on his tunic.

He held the Catholic faith in high regard. After all, it had originated alongside his own faith from the same region in the world and he found its symbolism quite fascinating.

Still! It wasn't an easy decision. He was putting a lot of trust into the future of their relationship, and the decision had not been reached without some growing pressure within their own situation.

The phone call, yesterday, from Cardinal Tolcini, announcing the arrival of an 'advisory envoy' the very next morning confirmed that the church could also see potential in their proposal, and affirmed just how much influence Francis held. It was looking promising.

Thorne Hex

The Rabbi stepped to the side door of the synagogue for the last time, switched off the light, and set the security system. He keyed in '8964,' and closed the door behind him.

Chapter 5
When in Naples ...

Moving to Naples had long been his ambition. Eight months in and Aldo was becoming more comfortable in the city.

His work as a freelance programmer served him well, and his new contract would enable him to relocate to a better part of the city.

The small café was unusually busy this morning, and the queue stretched out of the door and past the small cluster of tables set outside.

He decided to come back later and turned to squeeze past the people queuing behind.

Fate sometimes spins a cruel wheel – even when its greater purpose is not immediately apparent.

As Aldo turned, another customer passed briskly behind a waitress carrying a tray, catching her elbow unintentionally. She lost her hold on the tray, and several drinks dropped to the floor in a small cluster, splashing his bared legs and sandals with small smatterings of hot drink.

He limped and winced, and the waitress put a hand to her mouth, horrified at the accident unfolding in front of her.

An attractive girl, behind him in the queue put a hand on his shoulder.

'Are you alright?'

The waitress rushed to grab a cooled cloth to soothe his legs, and the girl helped him over to a stool and side bar table in front of the window.

The waitress arrived back with the dampened clean cloth, and the girl took it from her and began to dab at his legs, holding the cloth against his singed flesh.

She placed one hand onto his upper thigh, to steady herself entirely unaware of the effect it had on him, despite the pain.

'That was so brave of you,'

'What was?' He asked, bewildered.

'To step in and stop me being splashed, like that.'

'Oh! Yes.' He realised her assumption. 'You're welcome.'

She suddenly became aware of where she had placed her left hand. 'Oh! I'm sorry!'

'I can think of worse things.'

The girl giggled. 'I'm Allegro.' She offered her hand and he took it.

'Aldo.' He said, holding her hand.

The waitress stepped forward. 'I'm so sorry. Are you okay?'

'I'm fine. Really.' The cool cloth had soothed his legs, except for a couple of spots that still smarted.

'Let me get you both a drink. Please sit. I'll bring it over.'

Aldo slipped back properly onto his stool, and Allegra took the stool beside him.

'What brings you to Naples, my dashing hero?'

He blushed a little. It was pure chance that he'd turned at that moment.

'I live here now.'

Cult of the Dead

'Where are you from?'

'Switzerland. Near Zurich.' He didn't mention he was from one of the few poorer districts, or that his early life there had been very traumatic.

'Are you married?' She asked, cautiously.

Aldo looked at her, realising her interest might extend beyond merely thanking him.

He laughed. 'No. Do I look married?'

Allegra was very attractive. Her flowing dark hair was precisely and expensively braided, and even her simple clothes looked expensive and stylish.

Her smile held your eyes, and emphasised her good looks.

'What brings you here?' He asked.

'I work for myself and I have clients nearby.'

'What do you do?'

'I'm an accountant for small businesses.'

The waitress arrived with their drinks and some complimentary croissants, with jam and cream.

'Enjoy,' she urged, and went to help another waitress pick up the broken cups.

'Thank you,' they both said.

'Do you believe in fate, Aldo?' She asked.

He thought of a clever answer. 'Sometimes..' he told her. 'When it deals me what I want.'

She laughed. 'And what is it, Aldo - that you want?'

'Oh! The usual. A good life, no strife ...'

'Me too.'

'You didn't say?'

Allegra looked puzzled.

'Are you married?'

'Oh no!' She told him. 'I would if the right person came along, but I have yet to find him.'

He smiled. 'Perhaps a splash of fate will bring him to you?' He teased.

She laughed. 'Perhaps it will.'

Allegra reached into her bag and wrote down her name and number, handing him the small slip of paper.

'Here's my number. If you like, we can meet for dinner? We can test our fate together.'

'Thank you. I will.'

Allegra leaned forward and kissed his cheek. 'Thank you my gallant, Aldo. I have a client I have to meet in five minutes.',

She swept past him, pausing to put a hand back on his shoulder. 'Call me.' She whispered, and left.

Chapter 6
A New Soul

The new soul loitered indecisively in the greyness of the void. Never one for religion in life, it had no concept – no markers or signposts for where it now found itself.

At this stage, it knew nothing of the 'Soul-taking parties' that lurked in the void. No awareness of the many trials and tribulations it would have to endure, simply to continue existing in this dark place.

The 'White Teufel' approached slowly. This was a sensitive time for any new soul and its purpose was benevolent.

It recalled standing in almost the same spot, many years before. But in the void, time had small relevance.

When it 'spoke' it did so with its eyes. It invited the new soul to follow. As they walked, the new soul became aware that the kindly spirit was passing on understanding about the strange world in which it must learn to exist.

It took him to Purgatory – the place of waiting.

He led the new soul and read it. It hadn't been perfect in life – far from it. Sometimes selfish, often mean, this wasn't a candidate for direct entry to Heaven. It had much yet to learn.

It left the new soul at Purgatory. The new soul would be a little safer there. Not much. But some.

The hunting parties sent out from the foul wretches of hell did go there, but only when the pickings in the void were slim.

Better, and easier, to save energy and take captive souls from the void.

Once taken, few captive souls ever returned, for the Dark daemons fed greedily on their energy until they became so depleted they ceased to exist, in any form.

Death is not death until it is a depleted death. While there was energy there was existence, and while there was existence there was the hope of a reprieve.

Heaven, or Gan Eden was the only safe realm. But you could only be admitted with a pure spirit, when the lightness of your sin enabled a soul to rise up and be accepted.

'White Teufel's' had made the same journey successfully and had managed somehow to evade the pits and the traps of the Daemons.

Once purified and forgiven, they chose to remain below in the void helping others to begin the same test.

The knowledge they shared was granted from Heaven itself, and they became beyond reach of the Daemons and their sycophantic hordes.

The 'White Teufel' left the new arrival. From here it would have to find and choose its own path.

Chapter 7
Merit Park

The venue chosen for their meeting was called Merit Park.

The facility was the training centre for those entering military service as 'padres' in support of serving soldiers. Although it was predominantly focussed on the Christian faith, it was also an excellent setting for inter faith meetings, as it offered a subdued and simple form of Christian décor, making it seem more like a 'luxurious' Officer's Mess than a religious conference centre.

In addition to its very acceptable accommodation, it offered a level of security, with guards fully armed, when the threats in the UK or to visitors were high, but otherwise, it also offered magnificent grounds and conference facilities, and the centre was permanently staffed and catered for – even between courses.

He smiled at his own double-entendre as he recalled the excellent food and fine dining that was also provided alongside the training activities at the centre.

It had been Francis James's suggestion, and Cardinal Tolcini had found no difficulty in making the arrangements.

On the way, Father Ricci used the time on the aircraft to formulate some of his questions.

Thorne Hex

His mind turned back to a primitive Aramaic Code he'd explored during his long training as a Priest.

There was no evidence to substantiate the actual existence of any such code, but it might give them some 'common talking' ground, while they got to know each other. The task was sometimes used as an 'ice breaker' during training events.

It called for priests to identify 'core beliefs' matching 'religious significance' to each of the numbers from one – ten. He jotted his ideas down, marking out those he felt were shared by the two faiths;

- 1 – Belief in One G d / One True Faith.
- 2 – 'Nature,' the natural 'order. Two by two, Noah.

    3 – The Holy Trinity.
- 4 – The Four Cardinal Virtues – Prudence, Temperance, Justice and Fortitude.

    5 – The Pentagram [in demonology, a 'gateway.']

    6 – The devil / Satan as in '666', Hell, 'Sheol' and Purgatory.
- 7 – The 7 Deadly Sins - pride, greed, wrath, envy, lust, gluttony and sloth. [Proverbs].

    How / Are these reflected in the Mitzvot – the 613 'rules' given to Moses?

    8 – Historically a number symbolising 'eternity' in two parallel realms [two 'endless' circles].
- 9 – Good / G-d [Not pronounced / spelled in full in Judaism].
- 10 –The Ten Commandments – the Shema, the decalogue, Moses & Sinai.

Cult of the Dead

Overall, he felt that the little 'stimulus document' he'd put together emphasised how very much the two great faiths had in common.

Judaism, of course, he knew was much older than Christianity, dating back to about 2000 BCE or even 4000 BCE.

Judaism, Christianity and Islam all shared the same founder and ancestor in Abraham, - which is why they were often referred to as the Abrahamic Faiths, when considered and discussed alongside the others.

Jesus, on the other hand was born to a Jewish Mother, who some claimed was connected to very 'well placed' members of the Jewish priesthood.

But there was no particular place or role for Jesus in Judaism, and although believers in Islam regard Him as 'an important prophet,' Esau, in Islam, is just one amongst many prophets.'

The two men met in the lobby for lunch at 1pm.

Father Davide offered his hand. 'I see you are very well connected?' He said, looking around poignantly at their surroundings.

'I am blessed in many ways,' Saul conceded, and then countered 'But in the matter of connection, I always find there is just one that's truly important.'

Father Davide took to him easily. There was a quiet confidence about Saul that testified to a rich understanding borne from experience - not unlike himself. He liked his easy manner.

It would be fair to say that the matter of acceptance was probably settled favourably in the first two minutes of their meeting.

By the second day, Father Davide felt that he had gathered quite a full understanding of the candidate. He was well intentioned, and his easy manner, knowledge and experience would no doubt earn him the ready respect of his peers.

'There must be questions you have to put to me?' He asked Saul over breakfast

'Of course,' Saul replied. 'Thank you, please forgive me,' he continued, 'but what do you do, exactly?'

They both laughed at the unintentionally, comical nature of the question – given the many areas of personal belief and deeper thinking they had shared openly, already.

'You know what I mean,' added Saul.

'I work one to one, with some very deeply troubled clients,' Father Davide told him. 'My remit is for Naples, and the work is often 'sensitive' to say the least.'

'I see,' said Saul.

'It involves matters of life and death, and the interplay between those realms. But please don't discuss it elsewhere.'

'Of course.' Saul offered.

'Is that something that interests you?' Davide asked, breaking the momentary silence.

'If you mean the separate realms of the holy and unholy,' Saul told him, 'It interests me greatly in a theological way. But if you mean in any practical way, I'm not sure I'd be well suited. In the progressive branch of Judaism, we are more concerned with life and easing suffering in the realm of the living,' he said.

'Of course.' Davide conceded. 'It's not for everyone and certainly not for the faint hearted.' He intended no negative inference and none was taken.

In his head he earmarked Saul as a possible candidate for the field, much later, and recognised the man's immediate and great potential for challenging missionary work. He would be putting that in his report.

The Rabbi had an interest in the theological aspects of the work, and he knew his own abilities and limitations. He liked that. In his book, he was definitely the right kind of candidate for his own select field, and over time, he knew the church had a way of bringing such potential into play where and when it was most needed.

His mobile phone rang. He took it out and looked at the screen, apologising to Saul. It was Marilyn.

'Excuse me,' he said, and moved away from the table to take the call.

'Marilyn…How are you? It's been some time.'

He hadn't expected her to get back with news about the document quite so quickly.

'It has,' she agreed, 'but we're not doing apologies. Wow! What a find! How did you get hold of the document you sent?' She enthused. 'Where did you get it?'

'A client took it from a cult I've been looking at.'

'Wow, anyway….my first impression is that the paper looks genuine, but don't quote me yet. I am hopeful.' She told him. I've sent it away for formal verification. Police forensics have kindly offered to look at it for us, and the university will, of course.'

'Thank you, Marilyn. Thank you so much.' He genuinely appreciated her efforts.

'How long have we got you for?'

'I'm not sure. A week maybe.'

'Well, we are getting together' she told him. 'It's been way too long and we are not missing the window.'

'Agreed.'

'Send me your address details and I'll travel to you.'

'I will.' He promised.

'Oh!' She added. The document reference number is 'OSI 8964.' We don't want anything happening to this one, do we? Gotta' dash.'

Typical Marilyn! Here one minute, gone the next! She was always so full of energy – and busy!

He sent her his contact details so as not to forget later, and rejoined Saul.

'Bad news?' Saul asked.

'No. On the contrary, I'm hoping it will prove to be very good news.' Davide confided.

He told him in the very briefest way about the mysterious hidden cults of Naples – and without giving too much away.

After breakfast, the two men exchanged contact details, before going on their separate ways but very much as friends.

Father Davide had felt confident enough to let Saul know that his report would be entirely positive. Saul, in turn, had already invited him to attend the planned wedding and the reception, in just a week's time.

Father Davide knew from experience that jobs like this one could often be extended on the flimsiest of pretences, and he'd heard nothing more from Michela de Luca.

He concluded she was okay, for now.

Still, he'd phone her later, and check. Plans can be re shaped. They often needed to be.

It would also be a great chance to see Marilyn and he wanted to build on the promising connection with Saul.

Cardinal Tolcini could hardly complain. After all, he was giving the task his every earnest application.

It was Michela de Luca who had taken the old manuscript document before turning to him for help.

And, the demon had been quite right about that. She certainly was attractive! Not that he would break any of his pledges on the strength of something so fleeting or insincere.

He didn't judge his clients, as many were drawn to the occult by a deeper drive for understanding.

As a Priest of some standing, he was very much above giving way to the concerns of the 'flesh' – recognising how this would definitely impair his ability to intercede and would so much play to the strength of his adversaries – the demons.

He had found that the drawn-out nature of the exorcism rite often had to be adapted to respond to the different invading entities. This involved thinking on your feet, and working from a sure place of purity, within.

It was, in many ways, a battle of sheer will and faith between him and the dark spirits that presented before him.

Chapter 8
The George Restaurant

Allegra emerged from the taxi looking absolutely amazing. His heart beat faster.

He wondered if she would be embarrassed at the trousers and jacket he wore. It suddenly seemed quite 'boyish' - lacking anything of her apparent sophistication.

'You look lovely.'

'Thank you, darling.' She smiled and kissed him on the cheek.

'I'm so glad you chose not to wear a tie. It gets so hot in here, and I love that you've chosen a more casual look. Nobody likes a man who has to try too hard.' She smiled, and kissed him full on the lips.

'I was so glad to hear from you. I thought I might have put you off.'

He felt immediately at ease.

'Now! No arguments! I'm paying.'

'I could pay half.' He offered.

'No. I won't hear of it. You saved me from being scalded in the café and it's my treat.'

She hooked him by the arm and steered him towards the charming building. 'The views of Naples from here, are stunning and very romantic,' Allegra told him.

'Do you come here often, then?'

'I have been about three times, but only for special occasions. It's one of the best three-stars in Naples and the food is a creative delight.'

He smiled. He wasn't used to being so well treated.

The restaurant upstairs was exactly as Allegro had described. A large terrace at on one side offered a fabulous panorama of the Bay of Naples.

The waiter led them to an end table right on the end of the terrace with a superb outlook over the bay. You couldn't wish for a more romantic setting.

Aldo sat in one of the comfortable chairs, while the waiter tucked the chair in beneath Allegra. He looked at the traditional opulence that surrounded him. The ambience and informal chair made it very easy to feel you belonged there.

Allegra made it all so very easy. She played hostess, ordering the wine, and guiding his choice of food. It was like she knew he might be 'ropey' on those things, but she showed no open awareness of it, and she was so charming you couldn't have felt embarrassed.

'You have family in Zurich?' They were waiting for the wine to arrive.

'Not any more…' He tailed off.

'I'm sorry. What happened?'

'You might as well know from the start. My father was unwell and died, and my mother committed suicide a month later.'

Cult of the Dead

Allegra looked horrified. 'I'm so sorry,' she said again.

'It's okay. It was a while ago now.'

'So, you have no-one. No family, I mean?'

He shook his head.

'Then it's a good job we have found each other.' She lifted the mood again, smoothly.

The wine arrived and she tested it. 'Bene. Grazie.' When the waiter left, she lifted her glass. 'To us, darling.'

He raised a glass and they smiled before drinking.

'We spoke about fate…'

'Yes.'

'What do you really think about it?'

'I'm not sure. It hasn't always been kind to me.'

'I'm not sure either. But then it brought me to you…'

He smiled again.

'There are many other times when I think we make our own fate, don't you.'

'I guess. Why do you ask?'

'Some of my friends believe that you have to take an active role in creating your own fate.'

'That makes sense. I suppose I have - in coming to Naples.'

'How so?'

'After my parents died, I inherited a small amount of money. Enough to come here and make a fresh start. I have few good memories of Zurich.'

'I like you, Aldo.' She said suddenly. 'I don't want you to get the wrong idea. I rarely give out my number, but I like how you are, and I like that you have so much courage.'

He thought she meant stepping in front of the coffee splashes. 'Well actually…'

'I don't mean that. I mean that you have come here to Naples, all on your own, and you are carving out what you want, for yourself.'

'Oh!'

'My own life is very privileged. And so, I admire someone like you, who finds his own way.'

'Thank you.'

'You're welcome.' She smiled and they drank some more wine, taking in the views.

'What do you see in me?' She asked.

'I could easily ask the same. I'm surprised that you are interested in me.' He admitted.

'It's good that we are being honest. I find you very attractive, and that's very important to me.'

She leaned forward and took his hand.

'What do you like about me?'

'How you look. I like your style, and your easy way. I feel comfortable with you. You seem like someone I can trust.'

She smiled and leaned forward to kiss him over the table.

'Some people find me a little direct. I know what I like and I'm not afraid to show it. Some people find me overpowering and it's never made holding down a relationship easy.' She confided.

'I don't find you overpowering, and I like that you are open about your feelings. Are you like this with everyone?'

'Only when I find someone I really like. I'm just myself, mostly.'

The food arrived. It was everything Allegra had said it would be, and more.

After the meal they strolled a short way along the sea front, arm in arm. It was a beautiful evening.

'Would you think me awful if I invited you home, Aldo?'

He kissed her. 'Not at all. Is that what you want?'

'Yes. I do.' They kissed again.

'I would like very much for us to be together, and for more than just a night,' she whispered.

'I'd like that very much.'

She hailed a cab.

Chapter 9
The Five Realms

The daemon Squail inspected the surrounding mantle with his Marshalls in tow.

'See how it shifts.' He looked down to where the markings on the floor showed how the dividing mantle between the underworld and the physical plane had expanded by more than three feet, stretching, with its membrane taught and thin.

'You must ready yourselves, Marshalls. The time is coming.'

The four Marshalls nodded their agreement.

At the rate the mantle was expanding, it would soon be easy for any dark entity to cross back into the world of the living.

In his hotel room, Davide Ricci, leaned back on his pillows, dusting off the outer cover of a curious leather binder marked 'Memoires.'

He untwined the thin, leather laces that held the contents in place.

They were the private notes of Father Franco De Livre – the first Priest charged with the task of exorcising daemons at large in the community.

Davide had been meaning to read through them, having only glanced through them briefly.

Cult of the Dead

They contained single, handwritten notes compiled over many years. He placed them down on the bed and turned over the pages as one, to get to the first note, marking up the writer's many insights with a pencil.

Some of the notes were records of exorcisms. Others contained more thoughts and ideas about insights into the spirit realms.

He read;

'I do believe we find ourselves on the front line in the eternal battle between the forces of light and dark. In my fuller deliberations, I have given much thought as to what the gain of such a lasting struggle might be…'

Davide skipped down to the conclusions at the end of the note.

'It seems that the daemon's intention is to create as much dark energy as possible, and I can only conclude that the dark energy itself has purpose – else why bother?'

'I propose the possibility that the energy makes it easier for a spirit to pass between the confines of the living and the dead, in some way.'

About half way through the personal journal, he noticed a note about an exorcism performed on a lady called Francesca Montane.

Thorne Hex

'I was locked in mental struggle with the daemon, and it caused all the candles to extinguish with a violent rush of air that smashed the glass in the windows…'

'It was at this crucial moment that I noticed another entity standing just inside the pentagram…'

'In it, I sensed only the deepest regard and concern for me. There was nothing threatening about its presence. Indeed, I felt it was there to see that I was safe. There was the sense of a great pure energy about it nothing evil '

'My principle observations are two; I believe that there are 'good entities' working within the dark realms. I have named it a 'White Teufel' – and I believe it works for the forces of good.'

In my several engagements against occultist activities, I have observed that it does seem to be the Pentagram that is the 'requisite gateway' for daemons to pass into the real world, ordinarily.
My second observation is I suspect that it is not the only way. Perhaps, this is why some spirits have a greater need for dark energy.

He saw that his old mentor was proposing that there were two types of Daemon.

A 'Teufel' was like a free agent, moving freely between the under-realms and the physical world to carry out tasks on behalf of the resident Daemons that dominated the Underworld.

Both were powerful daemons in their own right. Just different - in their abilities and their roles.

Davide was reminded of the time when he had nearly died in a car crash. He was on an operating table in an emergency room, looking down at himself.

The machine readings showed that he had died.

He'd been drawn up into what he could only describe as a tunnel of brilliant light. A guiding entity had come to greet him and took his hands.

It was as if, in seconds, the guiding entity had read his soul, his life, his purpose and intention, and it began to urge him to follow it further along the tunnel.

He resisted. And the spirit took his hands again – wanting to understand more.

Davide had felt that in those swift moments, the spirit had imparted an understanding of where he was and what he had to do.

Then the spirit had nodded. It was as if it understood he had much unfinished business and the regard for another that needed him to be in the world of the living.

It released him, and Davide had opened his eyes on the operating table to see the medical team standing back with their fibrillatory plates, looking anxiously at the machines.

He shuddered. It had been a difficult time, and a long climb back to good, physical health.

Davide surmised that 'White Teufels' were essentially 'good spirits' that evaded the pitfalls of the underworld. They probably existed by exchanging help for energy until they reached a point where they acted as receptionist and guide to the newly deceased.

Eventually, they became so wise, powerful and able that they were virtually untouchable to the darker entities that filled the vaults of hell – or so it seemed.

He inserted a bookmark into the pages, and readied himself for sleep.

Chapter 10
Moving Forward Quickly

They met again for coffee in the café where they'd first met.

'Promise me you won't be mad?'

Aldo looked at Allegra, quizzingly.

'Mad about what?'

'Well…' She paused, choosing her words carefully. 'I know we have only just met, but I really worry for you being in this part of the city.

The Garibaldi district was close to the centre and within easy walk of the main rail station. By day, it seemed like just another district in Naples, but by night, it became home to hundreds of homeless people, who chose it as a temporary haven.

'I thought that maybe if you moved in with me, you could save the deposit for a better place more quickly, or you could just save the money and invest it, or something.'

'Really?'

'Yes. I worry about you being here at night, and my place is plenty big enough for the two of us.'

'I wouldn't want it to affect our relationship.'

'Nonsense, darling. It's a way for me to help you get on your feet properly. Besides we'll be together and I can curl up with you at night.'

'Are you sure?'

'Very sure. If you don't want to…'

'Of course, I want to.' He hugged her. 'Thank you.'

'I want us to be together.'

They drank their coffee.

'You'll be there tonight, won't you?'

'I'm nervous.' He admitted.

'There's nothing to be nervous about, darling. They're dear friends of mine and they are delighted to see me so happy.'

He looked unsure.

'Trust me. They'll help you. A lot.' She squeezed his arm, reassuringly.

'I'll be there.'

Chapter 11
The White Teufel

The White Teufel passed by the guards easily. Squail's minions were neither alert, nor diligent about their duties.

He joined the resting captives and sat next to one still recovering, taking both her hands. She was precariously weak and very close to dematerialising.

If that happened she'd be gone forever. Vaporised, instantly.

He placed a hand onto her forehead, gently, sweeping aside her hair to make a clear space for his palm.

The energy transfer was immediate, and a stronger light appeared behind the woman's eyes.

She went to thank him but he put a hand on her mouth, gesturing not to speak lest the guards should hear.

He was reminded of his many days spent wandering the under-realms avoiding the dark temptations and dark entities. There was much good in this one, he saw, and he'd help her. Perhaps she would survive?

He smiled at her, and then left as swiftly as he had arrived.

Chapter 12
Marilyn Forster

Marilyn stepped from the carriage as the train slowed to a halt at the end of a longer platform at Euston Station.

She slung the large hessian bag easily over her shoulder. It held everything she needed for a brief stopover and a meeting.

Marilyn happened to be glamorous and tall, and in slim and elegant proportions. Heads turned as she made her way through the turn-styles. She always looked good, but if she knew it, it didn't show, and was of no consequence to her, other than to present herself at her best.

Father Davide had opted to eat Greek. It was a tribute to them as their first connection had begun at the Mycenae Temple at Knossos, Crete, where they were both researching the ancient symbolism used by the Fertility Cult of the Bull.

He stood up to greet her, and she hugged him, warmly, as a dear friend.

'You look tired,' she chided.

'The joys of writing reports. You know how it is.'

She smiled and sat down.

He gestured to the proprietor, who came over, personally.

Cult of the Dead

'Hector, please can we have a bottle of your best red, and two large, whiskeys with ginger ale?'

'Of course, Sir.'

'So...' Marilyn glanced to him expectantly.

Davide looked momentarily puzzled, and shook his head slightly.

'Tell me!' She said. 'Where did you get it?'

'Ah! Of course. You want to know! Of course, you do! A lady, now a client, got involved with the cult, but quickly decided it wasn't for her. They forced her to take part in a ritual – or she felt she had to, at least. She pretended to pass out during the ordeal and they lay her down on a sofa in what looked like a study. The document had been left out with some other papers. She managed to take it without being noticed.'

'Very risky! What if they had cameras?' Marilyn asked.

'You're right. It was.' He agreed. 'But there hasn't been any indication of anyone going after her, so far.'

'No break-ins?'

'Not that I am aware of. Not yet.'

'Well! the good news is that the parchment and ink are both convincing. The ink is made from beetle blood and other additives, which is in keeping with the period.'

'Wow!' He said. 'Finally.' He picked up his whiskey and sipped, while he considered the implications.

'Does this mean you have a lead on the cult?'

'I'm not sure yet. I didn't want to push her too hard. Her brief involvement has already caused a lot of problems for her...but I am hopeful of something more from this.' He said.

'Let's hope.' She said.

'Come. Let's order.' Davide said. 'You must be starved?'

'Well actually...' Marilyn smiled.

'Oh! I meant to say,' he said, halfway through the starter, 'The document reference you gave me...'

Marilyn grunted her attention.

'It's exactly the same number as the PIN I use for my mobile.'

Marilyn caught the vine leaf starter that nearly slipped from her mouth. 'What?'

'Yes. It's a bit of a coincidence, isn't it?'

She nodded, and thought. 'What do you make of it?'

'I'm not sure. Nothing, I guess. It is quite a coincidence, though, isn't it?'

'Some sort of warning?' She suggested.

'It's not a very clear one, if that's the intention...and wouldn't they want the document back?'

'Someone trying to 'spook' you, maybe?'

They laughed, together, at the unintended pun – given Davide's work.

'Well, there's plenty of that going on,' he said, wryly.

'I'll come with you.' Marilyn said.

'What do you mean.'

'I'm due some holidays. I can give you a couple of weeks,' She offered.

'Well, yes! Wonderful. Of course. But there's a complication.'

'What?'

'I'm not sure when I'm going back just yet. Cardinal Tolcini seems all too happy to have me stuck here - out of his hair for now.'

'No problem. I'll just need to let them know at work, about a week before,' she said.

'Great. I'll let you know, as soon as I can.'

'Agreed.' She said, looking excited. 'I could do with a new challenge. It'll be like old times.'

Five courses and several more whiskeys later, and they hugged each other goodnight, before taking taxi's back to their own hotels.

It was like nothing had changed. They both felt rejuvenated.

Davide smiled to himself. He realised it felt really positive to have Marilyn back in his corner.

Chapter 13
Where Am I?

It was 5 am. Michela stood and stared at the Ovo Castle in Naples. She recognised it, of course. But she had no idea how she got there, why, or even when!

She sat down on a wall nearby. Shocked, and feeling very much alone. Tears formed quickly and she began to cry.

It was a full half an hour before she felt she could reach in her bag to call for a cab. Her phone was gone. So was her purse.

She sobbed mercilessly.

A passing postman spotted her and tried to console her without success.

It was only when the postal worker began to call for the police and for an ambulance that she felt able to pull herself together.

'Please,' she begged him, 'No police, or ambulances. Please, just call me a cab and I'll be okay.'

He looked at her doubtfully. 'Really.' She said. 'I have other money. I'll be okay.'

The driver of the cab that collected her was devoid of any sympathy, making her wonder what conclusions about her he had already reached.

She saw how he looked at her and watched her through his rearview mirror, but she didn't want to engage with him.

He didn't even try to conceal his irritation at having to wait for her to go to her apartment to get the fare.

Finally, she closed the door behind her and leaned back against it. Tears ran freely. She was exhausted, and very afraid.

She rang Father Davide's number on her home telephone.

Chapter 14
Between the Devil and …

Cardinal Tolcini was taking breakfast when Davide rang.

He listened carefully when Davide told him about Michela De Luca. 'I see..,' he said. 'I can get you a flight the day after the wedding.'

'Sooner!' Davide was insistent. He softened the response. 'She needs me there sooner,' he repeated.

'Davide, I understand your concern but you really cannot come back until after the wedding. We'll get a good man in there..'

Davide was furious. 'And when it goes to suicide, what then?' He said, barely concealing his rage. 'She's desperate,' he added. 'I need to be there now.'

'Okay. Okay. I see. I'll get you on a later flight immediately after the wedding. Nine O' Clock, maybe – depending what time the flights are available, of course.'

'Thank you, Cardinal.'

He could see he wasn't going to get past being at the wedding.

'I'll talk to Saul. I'm sure he'll understand.'

'I hope you are right about that.'

Cardinal Tolcini hung up.

Davide rang Michela De Luca, again.

'I'll be there as soon as I can be – the day after tomorrow,' he promised.

It took another hour for him to persuade Michela to give him her housekeeper's number, and her permission to ask that Chiara, her maid, should go and sit with her.

'I'll call you straight back, after I've spoken,' he told Michela.

Chiara agreed to be there at once. She was very fond of Michela and wanted to help.

'There's something else I need you to do,' Davide told her.

'Yes.'

'Get plenty of food in. Enough for four days, say, and buy two large containers of salt. I'll pay you for all the shopping.'

'Yes.' She said. 'I'm listening.'

'It's going to sound a little strange,' he said. 'But I want you to spread an unbroken line of salt along all the inside walls in her bedroom, and in the living room, bathroom and kitchen. All the main rooms you might be in. Get more salt if you think you'll need it.'

'I see. Can I ask why?'

'It is very difficult for bad spirits to cross.' He told her. 'It saps away their energy very quickly, and slows them down again on the way out. It's just a temporary measure, until I get there.'

He left her his contact numbers.

Chiara sensed his concern for Michaela, and trusted his intentions.

He rang Michela back. She seemed a little calmer now, and more reassured to know that he would be back with her soon.

'I remember having those awful dreams, again. I was fastened to a wooden cross and they'd put 'drips' in me. They were draining all my blood into large glass bottles right in front of me. I could see my own blood flowing through the tubes, into those awful bottles,' she told him.

He knew they called it a 'leaching' ritual, but he didn't tell her. 'I see. And then what happened?'

'I think I passed out. I'd been asleep on the sofa again. The TV reassures me.'

'And?'

'The next thing I recall is looking at the Ovo Castle. I mean, I was there – right in front of it, but I have no idea what happened in between. No idea where I had been. With who, or why? And…'

'Go on,' he said.

'My mobile phone and purse were gone. I don't know how or where that happened, or if I put them down, or if somebody took them?'

Her voice was starting to tremble again.

'Was any money taken from you?'

'No. I rang the bank and cancelled my cards and changed the mobile account. But nothing was taken as far as they could tell.'

They were after her address, he thought. 'Michela, listen. There's a Priest coming over to see you today. He's not likely to do the same kind of work as me, so please just use him to ask for any practical help you want. It's up to you how much you tell him – and Chiara will be there too....'

'I'll wait until you're back,' she said decisively. 'I'm not sure I'd want to tell a different kind of Priest about this.'

'Good. I agree.' He said. 'Thank you. Now, when Chiara is there, try to get some sleep. I've asked her to do something for me. It means putting some salt down, but it should stop you having those terrible dreams until I get back. If you need me before then, for anything, just call my mobile.'

'I will. Thank you.'

When Michela rang off, he texted Marilyn.

'Urgent. Cannot explain now but heading back the day after tomorrow. Join me as soon as you can. P.S. Please bring the document with you or ask the labs to send it on soonest. Needed. Best Regards & Thanks. Davide.'

Chapter 15
Let No Man Put Asunder

Davide rang Saul on the day before the wedding to arrange to call and see him. He explained that something 'sensitive and urgent' had come up and that he'd rather see him in person to explain properly – if only briefly.

Saul was pleased to hear from him and very happy for Davide to call by.

Davide left out the personal details and briefly explained a little more about trying to track down a mysterious cult in Naples. He said nothing of the exorcisms or 'black arts,' – having no wish to impact on the mood prior to the wedding.

Saul understood at once and said he was just very glad that Davide could be there for the wedding and at least some of the reception.

'I'll let you see the document when you come over to Rome.' He said. 'The funny thing was that the reference number for the document was the same as the PIN I used for my mobile – '8964.''

Saul looked surprised, and his mouth fell open a little.

'You won't believe this then,' he said, 'but that was the exact same number I used for the alarm system at my last synagogue.'

'No way! Are you serious? You're winding me up?' But he knew he wasn't. 'Wow! What are the odds?'

'Does that number mean anything to you – I mean other than being a security code?' Davide asked.

'Not really! I mean not directly to me.' He said. 'But didn't you say something about Aramaic Code when we were talking at Merit Park?'

'That's an interesting thought. Good thinking. Well, the 8 would mean eternity, the 9 would mean 'G-d' or good, the 6 would be the opposite of good, and the four would be the four Cardinal Virtues – Justice, Temperance, Prudence and Fortitude. It makes some sort of sense but it's not clear, what.'

'What about if you turn it on its side?' Saul asked. 'People use symbols in Kabbalah like that - which way up the symbols are shown changes their meaning entirely.'

'That would put the '8' over the '9,' which could mean 'Eternal G-d,' over the '6' which might represent evil. But I'm not sure where the "4" fits into that. Good thinking though. Thank you. Now, enough of that. You've got a wedding to prepare for. Oh! Yes. That reminds me...'

Davide handed him the beautifully wrapped gift from the Vatican – he guessed it was most likely to be the crystal cut decanter and glasses they stocked in the gift shop. A very nice gift – if he had it right?

He added his own personal gift of a large family Bible, a smaller Bible for Saul's own professional use, and two sets of Rosary Beads.

'Thank you, Saul, for being such a good man,' he said as they parted. 'I'm looking forward to tomorrow very much.' The wedding was scheduled for 12.30pm.

He thought some more about the code and the coincidences on the short tube journey back. It was getting a bit beyond 'coincidence,' surely? At what point does 'coincidence' become too much of a coincidence? He wasn't sure.

The wedding was so grand it was almost regal. Separate horse drawn carriages, brighter than white, delivered the groom first, followed by the bride exactly fifteen minutes later.

Francis escorted Sasha proudly down the aisle, and you could see by Saul's reaction when he turned to face her, that she was in every respect a resplendent and radiant bride.

Father Davide chose an end seat on the inside end of a long pew, on the groom's family side of the church.

It was during the exchanging of rings that two dark *Teufel's* stepped forward, *unseen*, from behind the Priest conducting the ceremony, and stepped smoothly into both the bride and the groom, through their backs.

Sasha looked down suddenly, just for a moment, and then forced the smile back onto her face. Saul just shifted uncomfortably for a moment. Of course, nobody noticed and if they had they would probably have put it down to brief moments of nerves. The bride and groom were only fleetingly aware of something, and neither party was going to let it spoil their special day by drawing attention to it.

Father Davide met Sasha for the first time when he was introduced on the way in to the reception. He liked her. She was every bit as warm, welcoming and easy going as Saul was. And most importantly, they both looked happy.

Davide felt you could always tell how well suited and prepared a couple were by how happy they seemed. They both radiated warmth to everyone, and their happiness was communicated through to all the guests.

It really was a splendid, convivial and warm occasion, and had the matter in Naples not been quite so urgent, Davide would very much like to have stayed for longer.

He watched Francis James doing his rounds, making sure that everyone was well attended to and that they all wanted for nothing. Davide couldn't recall when he'd last seen a father looking quite so proud.

Hindsight is a posthumous luxury, so to speak.

But the only part of the whole day that could be interpreted as 'off' was when the couple stood to cut the top tier on the seven-piece wedding cake.

Usually, couples removed the symbolic bride and groom straddling the top of cake before cutting into the top tier.

Davide had a keen eye for such detail, and most newlyweds wouldn't dream of separating the two figures. It would be like symbolically splitting themselves up.

Sasha, however, seemed to tug the knife over a little as they both held it, so that it sliced right down through the middle of the joined figures, and she turned, catching Davide's eye, just for a second, precisely at the moment Davide stood to leave.

Her eyes looked a cold, dark green rather than the blue, he'd noticed earlier. But he noticed the spinning disco ball suspended from the ceiling, which, he guessed, explained everything.

As for the iced figures – well, maybe they were just clowning around discreetly. Who knows?

He waved his way out to everyone and headed for the airport.

Chapter 16
Late

Aldo arrived at the Catacombs of San Gennaru with a single suitcase. He'd given notice on his flat and told the landlady he wouldn't be there for the duration of his notice.

'You can let it out earlier,' he told her.
She'd been good to him and it wouldn't hurt his situation any.

Allegro was late, unusually. He glanced at his watch.

He didn't notice the black Volvo with tinted glass slipping into the lay-by just behind him, until a large man got out and said 'Excusé.'

The man was dressed in a smart suit, and walked towards him, purposefully – as if moving closer before speaking.

Another large man alighted from the other side, a few steps behind.

'Yes?' Aldo said.

The man drew level with Aldo, and so did a van with an open side door. It screeched to an urgent stop just beside them.

The second man rushed up and thrust a dark hood down, roughly, over his head, and they manhandled him into the van.

He heard his case skidding across the van floor, alongside him.

Thorne Hex

One of the two man got in with him, and then he blacked out as the cosh hit the back of his head, hard.

When he opened his eyes, nothing could have prepared him for what he saw and felt.

Allegra and several other women, barely dressed, danced before him.

She released him from the fastenings that held him upright against a post of some sort.

Then she led him backwards and she lay down with her back on a stone slab.

She took a dagger of some sort from her toga, and made two small incisions in one of her forearms.

Allegra beckoned him closer and made two similar cuts in his arm.

The other dancing women then tied their arms together with cords - so that their blood mixed, and Allegra lay back, legs apart, pulling him into her and encouraging him to make love with her.

Suddenly, he was grabbed from behind, hauled and fastened tightly to a wooden cross – an 'X' rather than a crucifix.

The chord lines now cut into his wrists and ankles as he tested them to see if there was any movement.

A pentagram was engraved clearly on the platform he found himself stood upon.

There saw now there were lots of people watching from the floor space, with weird looking hoods on, in the half-lit surroundings.

Cult of the Dead

A man with a black, raven-like hood started to mutter in a language he didn't understand and had never heard anything like, before.

The line of five women now approached from the side and all then dropped their robes fully, while dancing naked around him and caressing his body.

His eyes widened and his mouth fell open as he saw Allegra was one of the five naked women.

'Allegra!'

She didn't acknowledge.

'Allegra,' he said louder.

'There will be a leaching,' boomed the man in a raven-like hood.

Allegra stepped forward.

Aldo's heart was pounding so loud he could hear it in his ears. His mouth was dry, and mortal fear held him almost frozen.

Her eyes seemed so detached – devoid of any feeling.'

His mind raced trying to work out what was happening, looking for some hope there might be a way out of his situation.

'Allegra.' His voice rose several tones as he tried to reach her, but there was no recognition and no response from her cold eyes.

She looked him, caressed his manhood, and skipped away from him, again.

The 'raven-man' handed her a sharp looking dagger, and she cut into his forearm twice, more. This time he cried out as he felt the dagger tip tear, rip, and gouge deeper into his tender flesh.

She squeezed his arm hard, forcing his blood into a goblet, before drinking some and letting some of it run freely down her chin.

They began to recite an incantation.

He felt numbed all over, and mercifully, the pain became briefly more endurable – even though his arm still stung.

He hung there dripping blood, while they invoked some dark entity and helped it rise up out of the floor.

Aldo's mind snapped, unable to comprehend what was happening. He began to whimper, and his legs shook visibly with fear.

He felt himself defecating, involuntarily.

The naked women danced on in front of him, caressing and touching him intimately, but that was now the very last thing on his mind.

Then, they took what looked to be 'drip needles' inserting the catheters into his arteries at the neck, his arms, and at the thighs. The last two were pushed into the tender flesh, either side, in his groin.

He shook with fear as the blood spurted forward quickly, filling the transparent drip tubes they fed into.

His mouth trembled and he whimpered.
'Please?'

None listened.

The giant glass vats his blood ran into were moved and they lined them up in front of him - where he could better see them filling.

Cult of the Dead

It took a full twenty minutes for the last of his blood to flow out of his body.

His eyes closed at fifteen minutes as the vital organs in his body began to shut down.

Allegro took hold of his unresponsive chin. 'Darling, how inconsiderate! You're no good to me – if you intend on always being so late! I think we should end things.'

She laughed to herself, and skipped nimbly away, leaving his white corpse suspended, while she left the stage.

Chapter 17
...Makes Work for Idle Hands

Michela offered another cup of tea.

He'd arrived just after Chiara got there, and introduced himself.

He was pleasant and helpful and had already made arrangements for yet another Priest to call by with some extra milk and the morning papers, the next day.

Michaela suspected the papers were more about him than her, but accepted his explanation that distracting herself with 'outside' matters might settle her mind, some.

'Yes, please. Thank you.' He said.

He watched with a measure of quiet surprise and disbelief as Chiara began laying an unbroken trail of salt around the inside walls of the lounge.

'For the mice?' He quipped, after a moment - somewhat bewildered.

Chiara wasn't offended. At least he had a sense of humour.

'Father Ricci's instructions,' she explained, and went through to the kitchen to make more tea.

'Oh! I see.'

In his early fifties, Father Enzo Gallo had none of Ricci's more extreme background. He'd come up through the traditional routes, first as a Parish Priest, and now as a Senior Administrator to Cardinal Tolcini.

He excused himself and went to the bathroom.

'Can I offer you something, stronger, Father?' Michela asked when he got back, and placing the tray of tea down on the elegant, marble-topped coffee table.

'Er, No. Thank you.' He said. 'Better not. Just the tea will be fine.'

She poured him a fresh cup.

'I must tell you that I'm nothing like Father Ricci. There's nobody else quite like him. My instructions are to look after you as best I can until he gets back.'

She smiled kindly at him. 'Father. I'm glad you are here, really.'

His eyes searched hers briefly, and he saw that she meant it.

'It's a comfort to me that you are here.'

'Oh! Good. Thank you.'

'I think probably the best thing is if I sit quietly and read my book.' He added. 'But if you do want to talk I will be very happy to do so. I am a very good listener.'

'There is something...' Michela began.

'Yes?'

She hesitated a moment. 'Can I ask.. do you ever question if G-d is there?'

'It may surprise you to know that as a younger man, I questioned everything, quite a lot. If you mean did I ever lose my faith or sense of direction, well, yes. Many times.'

'How do you find your way back?'

'I came to see that no matter how many times I questioned His existence, G-d never quite gave up on me. I found myself in many situations that would challenge most of us. I think G-d carried me through.'

Michela nodded.

'Why do you ask?'

'I think I lost sight of Him, for a time,' she said. 'And that's when the problems started.'

The loud scraping sound interrupted and startled them all.

They looked at Chiara who had just joined them, quizzingly.

Chiara shook her head and shrugged. 'It was from the utility room, I think.' Chiara leapt to her feet. 'I'll go.'

But Enzo was already ahead of her. 'Leave it with me,' he said, drawing a deep breath.

He stood in front of the open door to the utility room.

'I think you'd better come and see this.' He said, looking into the empty room.

Michela and Chiara looked at each other, and moved together, cautiously, along the hall.

When they drew nearer, the Priest stretched out his arm to push the inward opening door open fully.

Whoever had done this had to be behind the door. It was a simple cube shaped room. There was nowhere else.

He pushed the door deliberately, all the way back, expecting to feel a resistance. There was none.

Slowly he stepped into the room and leaned backwards, out of reach, craning his head to look into the blind spot behind the door. Nothing!

He stepped back and looked behind him to where the heavy washing machine had been scraped across the tiled floor.

Like everything else in Michela's flat, it was expensively decorated.

There were now four deep gouges in the floor tiles where the feet of the heavy machine had been pushed into the middle of the vacant room.

'Good G-d!' He exclaimed. Then, 'Forgive me,' as he recognised his own blasphemy.

It was Michela who broke their stunned silence. 'Chiara – more salt.' She realised that the utility room was the only space Chiara hadn't already salted.

She took the salt shaker from Chiara when she returned with it, and began to lay copious amounts on the carpet in front of the door space, and even tried to coat the top edge of the door frame.

She was surprised at how decisive and robust she felt – given the shock. But this needed action, not words.

She reached in and pulled the open door closed again, and all three of them moved back to the lounge having checked the salt lines were all completely continuous.

The three of them sat, side by side, staring expectantly along the hallway.

Father Enzo looked at each of them - now sat either side of him, on the sofa. He was suddenly very afraid, but put 'his face' on and began to recite The Lord's Prayer, over and over, getting louder and firmer each time – trying to drown out the incessant banging.

The dark *Teufel* Skallik, didn't need to go anywhere.

It sat, invisible but audible, astride the top of the washing machine and enjoyed banging rhythmically, on the sides of the appliance.

Chapter 18
The Gemonian Stairs

The utility of the Tiber as an instrument of drowning was well documented, historically and anecdotally.

However, its high, concrete, flood-barrier walls and a ban on swimming made drowning here a relatively rare occurrence in more recent times.

Detective Sergeant Rocco Costa crouched and studied the body at his feet.

It was unusual. He could see at once.

For a start, suicides didn't usually take the trouble to remove their clothing before taking the plunge, and somebody falling in accidentally would not have had the time to do so.

There seemed to be less bloating of the body than he'd encountered previously, perhaps suggesting it hadn't been in the water too long. The autopsy would tell him more.

Two aspects caught his attention quickly. The discolouring of the body was not as uniformly spread over most of the body, as he might expect.

On the reverse side it was almost bruised in its complexion, while the front side was pale and grey-blue.

Something else happened to this one before it entered the water.

There were also four strange cuts on the inside-right forearm. Two sets of parallel cuts – presumably made with a knife, were quite shallow. The other two looked deeper and messy – as if cut with a jagged blade.

There were also some tight, residual cord marks above and below the incision points, and also at the ankles and wrists. Different widths of cords though?

And bruising on each side of the neck and in again in the groin. They looked almost medical? But why? From what?

The absence of clothes or any other forms of identification was not going to help much with identifying the victim.

He looked around at the discovery point. There were no obvious signs of struggle nearby and as the body had been spotted bobbing in the water by someone walking a dog, he judged it unlikely they'd get much help from the scene itself. Still, he'd leave forensics to get on with it, just in case.

Historically speaking, the Gemonian Stairs led down to the Tiber past the ruins of the Mamertine Prison.

The steps, he knew, had been an execution site where criminals, and sometimes others, were strangled and left on the stairs for wild beasts to devour, before their remains were slung into the Tiber to make room for more.

The features of the corpse did not look typically Roman or Italian, but it was easy to be mistaken about that.

Cult of the Dead

He borrowed a pair of scissors from a nearby Scene of Crimes worker and cut a small sample of hair from the corpse. He'd probably need to pass this up to Interpol to help with identification.

The autopsy report would follow in due course.

He'd estimate the victim was in his early to mid-twenties. He had been in reasonably good shape, physically, from the outside, at least.

He signed the despatch paperwork to allow the body to be moved when forensics had finished, and went back to his car.

There was distinct oddities about this one.

The chord marks and cuts aroused his suspicions naturally, but he'd have to wait for more confirmation from the lab.

The body colour was very different to other drownings, too. Much whiter, somehow.

It was quite unusual to be called to a body in the river, these days. Swimming was banned. Besides this man looked healthy, and few people in Italy don't swim. It was almost a part of the culture.

Chapter 19
The Cult of the Summoned

The demon Squail was truly grotesque – even by demon standards.

In the world of dark spirits, power and evil are expressed, in part, through distortions in the way that a spirit appears to others.

Squail was permanently stooped and rickety. The knee caps had become so distorted that they struck out at almost ninety degrees to its legs so that its stooped, twisted trunk sank even lower.

When Squail walked, the oversize knees bounced up slightly higher than his dropped hips, adding a beetle-like, scurry to its awkward gait.

Browned, ancient skin was gnarled and stretched so tightly over the bone structures that in places it became almost transparent. You could see the pulsing movements in the veins and arteries as the energy surged around its body.

In other places, such as the points of the elbows, the front of the trunk, and the shoulders and neck, long globules of brown flesh hung down oddly from the brown torso like collapsed haemorrhoids.

Its skull shone through its face in the places where the wrinkled, brown flesh was most stretched. Elsewhere, shards of surplus flesh slopped down in long, tubular sacs like the ugly, long skin tags you sometimes see hanging off the heads of old turkeys.

The eye sockets were set back so far into the face that you had to watch carefully for an occasional movement of the eyelids, to spot the tiny red pupils that provided the only confirmation there were eyes there, at all.

The lobes on each ear dropped down so that they almost met with its shoulders.

The overall effect gave a strange impression of a lump of streaked, chocolate marble, wrought into the form of a twisted, ancient, brown mole – more mole than human.

The worst aspects of its appearance were the enormous stiletto-like tongue that flicked at its own lean lips, and the flowing strands of phlegm, mucus and slime that dribbled incessantly from its nasal orifices, while it slabbered from its mouth.

Occasionally, as it walked, Squail swept up a strand of dripping mucus up with two fingers - passing it deftly over to the opposite arm and suspending the strand temporarily from a robe sleeve, while flicking away the excess with a snappy, sideways flick of its knobbly fingers.

It would soon be time for Squail to depart.

There was no mistaking the 'draw' felt by a demon when it was summoned by name through a portal.

Squail stepped forward to where the last line mark on the floor revealed the mantle's most recent expansion.

It was as if the membrane of the mantle suddenly swept around him, and he stepped into it willingly.

The demon stepped out, and upwards, into the centre of a Pentagram surrounded by a sea of hooded faces, each holding a single candle.

'Kneel,' Squail commanded, stepping up into the Pentagram. 'Who summons, Squail?'

'I did.' Said the Dark Raven, stepping forward, one step, boldly.

He was readily distinguished by a beaked, black hood, that covered just the upper half of his head. The ritual leader smiled a welcome.

'Come, Great Raven.' Squail said. 'Join me here – within our circle. We will address them together, as one.'

Such instant approval and recognition were rare and a great honour indeed.

The Raven moved towards the demon, eagerly, ready to take his place.

Squail held his arms aloft in a grand gesture of greeting, and then suddenly lunged forward consuming and absorbing the Raven into itself, all in one movement.

A couple of symbolic feathers from his Raven shawl danced their way slowly down to the floor, - the only physical testimony to his former existence.

Cult of the Dead

'Ahh! Fresh Raven. How lovely!' Said Squail, enjoying the moment.

The gasps were fully audible. The fear in the room, suddenly all-consuming.

A few rose to their feet, eyes and mouths wide open in disbelief.

'Kneel.' Squail ordered. 'Silence.' 'Foolish serfs. Did I not just tell you we'd be speaking to you, as one?'

Squail began to chuckle loudly, enjoying the demonstration of its power, and dark, lashing humour.

The mucus streams began again.

He swept two fingers out to catch the rapidly forming strand and flicked it nimbly onto the hooded faces of three or four cult members, kneeling just off to his right.

They turned their heads away in disgust, repulsed by the pungent, foul stench that invaded their nostrils quickly - through their white cotton hoods.

'I honour you,' Squail told them. And laughed more still at their humbled, shock and revulsion.

'Your astonishment is pleasing to Squail. Now. Listen carefully. There must be no mistakes. There will be a high price to pay for those who fall short. Get it right, and I will feed you all the power you ever dreamed of. From now on, you serve only me.'

Squail held their full attention.

Chapter 20
A Safe Haven

Father Davide knew something was wrong when all three of them opened the door as one.

Michela and Chiara had also stepped back much further along towards the lounge than was actually needed.

'Hello Father Enzo,' he said, recognising the administrator right away. 'Thank you for being with them.'

They had spoken many, many times previously, but neither would have claimed to know the other well.

Michela stepped forward and hugged him. 'Thank G-d you're here.' She looked at Father Enzo. 'Thank you, both.' She added.

Chiara said 'Hello,' and nodded, smiling weakly.

'It's in there, Davide...we think.' Enzo told him, gesturing towards the closed utility room door.

'What is?' He asked.

'It. Whatever it is?'

Davide put his bag down and ushered them towards the lounge.

'Tell me.' He said. 'All of it.'

He listened diligently while they told him what had taken place.

'But we've heard nothing more since about thirty minutes before you arrived.' Enzo said. 'We just kept praying, until we heard the doorbell.'

'Chiara, do we have any salt left?' He asked suddenly.

'Yes, Father. We should have. I brought a pack of six.'

'Thank you. Wait here,' he said.

He got up and went to the kitchen before returning to the door by the utility room. He waited, there in the hallway, listening. Nothing.

After several more minutes, he gently opened the door a touch and then pushed it fully open.

There was nothing strange to be seen other than the washer in the middle of the room and the damage caused by the scratches.

He moved quickly, opening the salt container as he entered the room. Father Davide began to seal around the inside base of the walls with an unbroken line of salt.

The *Teufel* was still there, watching. It just wasn't visible. It left through a wall before the salt barrier could be completed.

Father Davide checked his work and then stepped carefully over the unbroken line crossing the doorway.

In the lounge, he said, 'Ladies. You'll need to pack a few things. Enough for a few days. Father Enzo, would you be good enough to accompany me back in the taxi when the ladies are ready? I'd like you to stay with us overnight, as well, if you will?'

He nodded his agreement.

They travelled in silence for the first few minutes. Davide looked around to where Michela sat looking through the side window from the seat behind the taxi driver.

'If it didn't leave already, it won't rush to go back in there while those salt lines are in place.' He told her.

A few minutes later the taxi turned into the street leading up to the 'Centre.' It stopped outside. It was when they got out of the cab that they saw it.

Across the concrete lintel bridging the door, someone had daubed 'Condemned' in a kind of red paint mix. There were a number of other 'messages' dabbed in the same paint and probably with the same brush but done with different hands.

'How utterly brainless,' Davide said. 'There's nothing wrong with the building by the way. Ignore it, please.'

He realised that it wasn't 'brainless,' of course. Far from it. The building was fine. He was sure of that. But they had no idea if the culprits were mortal or spirit, and their graffiti sent out the striking messages that whoever it was, knew exactly where they were - and that they had the ability to reach them.

More, one of the daubed messages was the number; '8 9 6 4.'

Somebody, or something was playing 'mind games.'

He held his own counsel, saying nothing, and led them all inside.

Chapter 21
Thought, Word, Intention & Deed

After the wedding, many of the guests stayed on at the hotel with the bride and groom and their family.

Saul liked that. It had been Sasha's idea, and although he wasn't entirely smitten by the idea to begin with, Saul had to admit that it was very relaxing to have a couple of extra days there, surrounded just by people they knew well, before jetting off on their honeymoon.

People weren't intrusive at all and mostly did their own thing. It also gave him some rare quality time with Sasha's family.

He joined Francis James on the front terrace, for breakfast. Sasha wanted to sleep in a little.

'Good morning.' Saul said pulling up a chair.

'Good morning.' Francis responded, peered over his paper. He folded it, and placed it down on an empty seat.

'Is Sasha joining us?'

'Maybe later,' Saul told him. 'She wanted to sleep on some.'

'She had a few, last night, didn't she?' Her father said. 'Still! I was surprised.'

'Surprised?'

'She told me that she didn't want religion dictating your lives together,' Francis said. 'She can be a little direct, sometimes.'

'Yes, she can,' Saul conceded.

'I haven't mentioned it to Mary. She wouldn't take it well. Did she say anything like that to you?'

'Not that I recall.'

'Good. Perhaps she just had a few too many. It was her big day, after all.'

Mary came out of the hotel and looked around for them, before heading across to join them.

'Anyway. I'm sure you can handle it, but I thought it might be better if we kept an eye on it between us.'

Mary joined them before he could respond.

'Good morning,' she said, smiling.

Saul knew that this was how things 'worked' in the James family. Things were communicated independently, but he had no doubt at all, that the matter would have already been discussed in every detail between Francis and Mary. They were very together.

He didn't resent it. It was all a part of what made them so successful.

'Good morning,' he replied, to Mary. 'I'm hungry.'

'I am too.' Mary said, and laughed.

'While you are both together, I just wanted to thank you for yesterday. It really was an unforgettably special day.' Saul said. 'Perfect in every way. Thank you.'

'Not at all.' Mary beamed at him, even so. It was nice to feel appreciated, and Saul might bring a little more of that into their family unit, she hoped.

Francis grunted his agreement.

Saul studied the breakfast menu. If Sasha had intended the comment in the way it had been reported, he did wonder how it was going to fit in with his plans to change his faith. He'd have to bring it up at some point.

They ordered the food.

'Good Lord!' Francis said, unexpectedly.

They followed his gaze to where you could see just past the building to part of the causeway at the front of the hotel.

A taxi had pulled up, and the person getting into the back of it looked very much like Sasha James.

'I'm sure there's a perfectly ordinary explanation,' Saul said, wondering, at once, why Sasha hadn't thought to mention it?'

Chapter 22
Aldo Fiore

Two weeks had lapsed since Rocco Costa had checked over the body in the Tiber. But he'd not been idle.

Interpol had been really quick getting reports back to him.

Aldo Fiore, the victim, had joint Swiss-Italian citizenship and was twenty-three years old.

He was a young man who had already suffered considerable disadvantages in his own way.

There were no criminal connections or irregularities in his background checks that indicated any involvement with drugs or less savoury aspects of lifestyle.

He was in all respects a model citizen so far as Rocco could tell.

There was a report from a neighbour, in Naples, that Aldo had recently met a very attractive girl called Allegra. But he could not make any more progress with that line of enquiry as nobody else knew who she was, or anything much about her.

The most curious aspects came back in the pathology report.

It seemed that somebody had very kindly emptied out most of Aldo's blood supply before dropping him in the river.

His own focus was now very much in trying to discover the connection with the curious marks and cuts on Aldo's forearm.

He was leaning towards some sort of ritualistic killing, but so far Cardinal Tolcini, at the Vatican, had only been able to make a vague connection and suggestion that the strange cuts might indicate occult activity.

It all seemed to be a bit of a 'dead end.'

And that was something Rocco Costa felt very strongly about.

When apparently innocent young people were getting killed in bizarre ways, it meant that the streets were potentially unsafe for a lot of people.

Occult crime was on the rise in Rome and Naples, and the police and the Vatican were discovering there was much to be gained by sharing their knowledge.

He rang to speak with Cardinal Tolcini again. He wanted to know what he was dealing with - and why a person living in Naples might end up floating bloated and dead in the River Tiber, in Rome?

Chapter 23
Next Steps

The inside of the 'Centre' was well-suited to its purpose. It predated most of the surrounding industrial units and had originally been built as a large warehouse for the storage of grain, before being modified to become an ancillary district headquarters for the Vatican.

Originally, intended as a grain distribution centre for use in times of famine, the modifications included a separate wing with sleeping accommodation for the Swiss Guards and staff who might occasionally be asked to stay there for quite some time.

It also boasted supporting facilities like a small commercial kitchen, male and female rest rooms, separate male and female shower and washing facilities, and a number of interview rooms, as well as the main hall most frequently used by Davide, for exorcisms.

He showed them all to a room each, and then went into the kitchen to make drinking chocolate for everyone.

Part of the main hall was set up as an open plan 'lounge' and discussion area, and there were plenty of side rooms that could easily be adapted to other purposes.

Davide had already set up one of the side rooms as a Television room and Reading Room, in case a client should ever need 'shielding' for a sustained period.

The main hall was encompassed by a mezzanine terrace with administration and records offices already in place around the rectangular walkway. Access was via short, straight staircases at either end, and in the middle on each on longer side.

The original warehouse beams had been retained, giving the building a stylish, medieval feel to it. There were far worse places to be confined to.

He carried the drinks through on a large tray, and his guests naturally 'gravitated' back to the main seating area in the hall, once they had settled in.

The sleeping accommodation was at the back of the building and the back walls in each room were part of a larger outer wall, without windows, forming the back to the small compound surrounding the building.

Anybody or anything climbing at the back, would find themselves on a flat, hard roof with absolutely no access points to the sleeping quarters.

Unfortunately, this did give the rooms the appearance of being like large cells, but right now it was ideal – as the only routes in were through the front, or directly through the walls.

When they were all settled, he gave them a few minutes to adjust to their new surroundings.

Cult of the Dead

'Chiara and Michela, I wondered if you mind helping by ordering in food for the next four or five days?'

The two ladies looked at each other and then nodded.

Davide took an account card from his wallet and handed it to Michela. 'Thank you. If you order through the telephone number on the card, or use the internet, the cost will go straight onto the account.'

'Father Enzo. I thought you and I might keep first vigil? But before we do, we'll need to salt the perimeter. Some of it will probably get washed or blown away, but it seems prudent while the drier weather is yet with us.'

Father Enzo agreed.

'After that,' Davide said to everyone, 'It's probably best if we don't go outside at all, for the next few days. But if we do have to, we should be in pairs.'

'I'm hoping one of my colleagues will be able to join us in the next few days.' He told them.

'I suggest that when our immediate tasks are done, we should all try and get some rest. With salt down, I hope you all find you sleep better.'

When the two priests returned from laying down salt, the two ladies had retired.

'Thank you, Enzo. I hope you'll get some rest too.'

'I'll do my very best,' he said, and retired to his own room.

Davide decided there was no point in them both staying awake. He knew his mind was too active for sleep.

He took a piece of paper and a pen from his desk area in the corner of the main hall. He wrote '8 9 6 4' on it, and studied it for a moment. Then he wrote;

8

9

6

4'

vertically, instead.

There was something about the second way of writing it that caught his attention. When it was read downwards it was almost like a diagram of the 'spiritual realms' – with 'eternal' and 'heaven' being represented by the '8 & 9,' set above 'the dark realms' – the '6'. That kind of made sense. So, what was the '4' all about, he puzzled?

The usual Christian meaning attributed to the '4' would have been either just the word *'for,'* or the *Four Cardinal Virtues – Justice, Fortitude, Temperance and Prudence* – but that didn't much help.

Cult of the Dead

It was obviously cryptic. He thought about what it could mean if viewed from the underworld.

There was no strict opposite to the four *Cardinal Virtues*. The closest to opposites he could think of would be the *Seven Deadly Sins*. He wrote them down;

The Seven Deadly Sins - *pride, greed, wrath, envy, lust, gluttony and sloth*. [The Book of Proverbs].

He reorganised them into those that seemed to go '*hand in hand.*'

Greed, envy, gluttony, all sat well together, as they could all be a part of the same set of emotions. That left *pride, wrath, lust* and *sloth* for the other group.

Treating '*greed, envy and gluttony*' as the same thing, that left him with '*greed, wrath, lust and sloth*' – represented by the '4.'

It seemed to fit – in a way, but it still didn't quite explain the number code, fully?

That could be a part of it, he concluded, but it had to be something else. Something a bit more transparent, when you saw it.

He put the paper down and went to make coffee.

When he came back to it, he was fairly convinced that the '8 9 6' part of the code represented the juxtaposed 'Heavenly realm' and the 'Dark realms' beneath. The '4' was obviously critical to unlocking its more complete meaning.

'What is its purpose of the code?' He asked aloud.

He wrote, 'curiosity, mind-games / power-play, warning [friendly], boasting / taunting [hostile], intimidation, 'red herring / deception.'

Then he remembered that the number had been daubed on the wall outside, along with the other messages. There was no way that was an act with any friendly intention about it. Why daub it on the wall?

That left *'mind-games, boasting and intimidation'* – unless it was intended as a *'red herring'* – all of which fitted very well with what he had experienced as a part of *demonic modus operandi*.

The more he thought about it, the more it made sense from that perspective alone. It wasn't conclusive, but he felt sure that when they worked out for sure what the '4' was about, it would all make much more sense.

He looked at his watch. It was 6 am. He'd intended to let Father Enzo sleep on, anyway. He fetched himself more coffee.

Chapter 24
Cracks Turn into Fractures

In the five years they'd been together, Saul and Sasha rarely fell out.

If a decision had to be made quickly, it was governed by what was the most pragmatic outcome available to them.

Whenever they did disagree strongly about what that should be, they tended to withdraw quickly to their corners, and then look to find an acceptable solution and compromise later.

When Sasha got back, Saul asked her about the journey she'd taken in the taxi and the comment she'd made to her father. Things escalated very quickly.

Sasha implied that she didn't much care for him working with her father to decide what was best for her.

There had been a simple explanation for her unannounced excursion. She was carrying it in the shopping bags she came in with! Sasha had wanted to top up her wardrobe with a few bits and pieces before they set off for Italy.

Saul pointed out that it didn't explain why she hadn't mentioned her plans.

Sasha reasoned that trust shouldn't be an issue at this stage, and retreated to 'her corner.'

Unusually, Saul went to the bar, having told Sasha that he felt she was being most unreasonable.

He ordered himself a strong drink and retired to a comfortable chair to consider his position, in solitude.

An attractive guest walked into the bar area and said 'Good Afternoon' as she passed.

He was surprised. People often didn't, these days. She smiled at him, warmly, and went to the bar.

He was deep in thought when she arrived back at his side, drink in hand.

'You look like you need some good company,' she said, 'I'm Annabella.' With that she sat in the chair next to him.

'I'm really not sure…'

She beamed at him, again, holding his gaze, steadily with rich, green eyes that he unexpectedly found very attractive.

'Nonsense.' She said, resting a hand briefly on his knee. 'You just need someone to bring out the best in you. Now. What are you called?'

'Saul,' he told her.

'Sexy name,' she said. 'I like it.'

There was something very appealing about her confident charm and easy manner, and her eyes were amazing. He knew he was feeling vulnerable. He'd finish his drink with her and go, he decided.

Of course, it didn't quite map out that way. He finished his drink ahead of her but found that he was very much enjoying her conversation - and the large massage to his bruised ego.

He didn't feel ready to go back to talk with Sasha, just yet, so he offered her another drink and she accepted.

It was also something of a shock to discover that as true as his feelings for Sasha were, there was no denying that he also found Annabella very attractive.

He excused himself while he went to the gents.

When he returned, Annabella had lined up some more drinks on the table.

They'd reached the point in their conversation where Annabella wanted to know more personal details about who Saul was and what he was doing there.

He told her that he'd got married yesterday, and that as much as he was enjoying her company, he didn't want any of the other guests who had stayed over from the wedding, and who knew him, getting the wrong idea.

'We can go somewhere a little more private if you like?'

She rested a hand on his thigh and left it lingering for a moment or two. Saul found himself getting unexpectedly aroused.

She sat back and took out a pen and piece of paper from her clutch bag and scribbled 'Room

115.' She turned it over and scribbled a mobile number, signing it 'A' with a flourish.

'I'm sure we could both get to know each other much better over a glass of Vintage 69, or two.' She said.

With that, she finished her drink and left, giving him a gentle kiss on the cheek. 'I'm here for a couple of days,' she said, 'but you can use the telephone number at any time.'

The encounter unnerved him. He ordered another drink and sat down again, acknowledging the truth of his own feelings.

He had felt real lust. He recognised thoughts, feelings and intentions in himself that he'd really been strongly aware of before. As much as he tried not to, he found himself thinking about those amazing eyes.

He screwed up the note, but then put it into his pocket, anyway. 'I'll drop it in the bin later,' he thought, but somehow he thought he might not do. Not just yet.

When he got back to the room, Sasha was already in bed, and asleep, or pretending to be. He showered and changed, before climbing quietly into the bed next to her.

He went to sleep thinking of 'amazing green eyes.'

Chapter 25
Rising to the Challenge

The arrival of Marilyn lifted the mood at the centre. She quickly forged friendships with Michela and Chiara, and Father Enzo was fascinated by their long conversations about religious practices and artefacts in different faiths and cultures.

Father Ricci felt that it was time to start tracking down the Cult of the Summoned.

He had just returned from the early evening business of topping up the salt perimeter with Father Enzo, when he caught up with Marilyn and Michela in the kitchen.

'Good evening, Lady's. How are we tonight?'

They seemed quite buoyant, in the circumstances, and Davide said so.

'Michela..' He paused, feeling guilty and wary about steering her thoughts back to her recent traumas.

'It's fine, Father. Really.' She sensed his discomfort, and she was very perceptive. She knew there would be a need for further discussion. 'Ask.'

He looked at Marilyn, who made no gesture either way.

'The night you ended up at the Ovo Castle,' he said. 'Is there anything more you can remember?'

She thought hard, for a moment.

'It's a complete blank from about 10 pm the night before. Chiara had been with me until about 6 pm. I read a little and watched some television. Then I felt tired and went to bed early.'

'Were there any phone calls?' He asked.

'It did ring,' she said. 'But it rang off before I got to it.'

'What time was that?'

Quite late. About 9 pm, I think.'

'I was in the kitchen and it rang several times before I realised. By the time I got there it had stopped. There was no number. It was withheld by the caller.'

'How many times did it ring?

She thought, again. 'Eight or nine, maybe?'

'I see. Thank you. Changing the subject, a little, the night you went to the cult meeting, how did that happen?'

'I'd met with an old friend in the Café Roberta. We hadn't seen each other for years. We had coffee together, and got chatting. She'd asked if I still attended the local church group, and I told her how I felt it was no longer meeting my needs.'

'So, she brought it up - the questions about the church, I mean?'

'Yes. I'm sure, or I wouldn't have discussed it.'

'Go on…'

'That's when she told me about this group that was really different.

She said that they'd been around for some time, but they were very selective because the Holy

Church wouldn't like the way they were exploring new ideas and making ritual really meet what people needed.

Then she gave me her number and a number to call if I was interested in going to see what they did at the meetings.'

'And then what happened?'

'Nothing, right away. It was about a week later and Chiara was away. I thought why not just take a look?

'I rang the number she had given to me, and a man answered. He seemed really helpful. He said that the meeting place could be difficult to find, if you didn't know it. So, we met at a Pizza place near to an 'Artsy' part of the city. It seemed to take a lot longer to get there than I expected. When we set off he said it wasn't too far. I think, maybe, he took me down lots of little streets so that I wouldn't easily remember. I do remember passing a really colourful building. It had lots of pillars at the front of it, and they were all brightly decorated.'

Marilyn had been listening. She reached for her laptop and began searching while Michela explained.

'When we got near he said I'd need to cover my eyes, and he gave me a headband. It didn't stop me seeing everything, but it made it difficult to see clearly. Then he left me! I panicked a little, and took off the headband. I was only there for a few seconds when a different man introduced himself. He knew my name and he led me to some steps that led into the back of one of the buildings nearby. Then it got even more weird.'

'How so?,

'Well, they introduced me to a few of the main people in the group, and they said I was very fortunate as I'd have a chance to see them practicing for a special ritual that they only do occasionally. It seemed a bit odd. People don't usually need to practice for a church service, do they?

Father Ricci nodded. 'That's an interesting point.' He said.

'They took me into what I thought would be a church of some sort. But it was more like going to an opera. There was a balcony overlooking the main room, and there were lots of people gathered there. But then I saw the Pentagram, and I got scared. It looked like they were going to do some kind of witchcraft, or something. And the only light was candlelight. That made me even more nervous. Since when do you burn all of your candles for a practice?'

'What happened then?'

'They all knelt down and a man at the front said some prayers in a language I've never heard before. When I asked, a guy next to me whispered that they teach you the language when you join them. They all pulled up these white hoods that were fastened to their tunics. I decided I'd had enough, so I pretended to faint. It seemed easier than explaining I didn't like what they were doing.'

'What did they do, then?'

'The guy at the front came over and looked at me. He took off his mask and he had the weirdest eyes. He slapped my cheeks on either side, trying to bring me round. I made out I was still groggy and confused. A couple of them carried me out and took me into a large office, next to the temple. It was a bit like a study, with lots of old books and objects on the shelves. They lay me down on a sofa and put a cushion under my head. One said he'd get some water, and the other said he'd speak to the chief, and they just left me there. That's when I saw...' She stopped talking for a moment, and looked at Marilyn and then back to Father Ricci.

'It's okay he told her. You can trust Marilyn.'

'That's when I saw the piece of paper, with some other bits and pieces. I was curious about the rhymes and I thought it might tell me a little more about what they do. But I also realised it might be my best chance to sneak out, so I took the paper, the one I gave you, and left. They were all still busy doing the ceremony, and I was able to get out quite easily.'

'Did anyone come after you?'

'Not that I saw,' she said. 'But I just wanted to get away. So, I ran until I found a main road. I had no idea where I was. I just found a taxi and left as fast as I could.'

'What made you call me?' He asked her.

'I started having the dreams I told you about. Those terrible dreams. They scare me. I tried sitting up, taking sleeping pills. Nothing stopped them. It was making me ill.'

'Thank you, Michela.' He said. 'I think we've learned enough for now. Would you like some more tea?'

Michaela nodded and he went to the side of the kitchen to make some.

Marilyn stopped what she was doing and pushed the computer away. 'Are you okay?'

She moved around the table and gave Michaela a hug. 'You're very brave. The piece of paper you found, we think is genuine, and it might help us to show that these people are real and are involved in some very worrying things.'

Michaela nodded.

'We have to prove they exist and we need to show what they are doing so that the Church will get involved. Everything you've done may stop a lot of people getting hurt. Thank you.'

She hugged Michaela again and held her hands.

Father Davide brought over tea for everyone, and asked about Chiara, and how long Michela had known her.

Marilyn was at her very best, and told Michaela all about how she had first met Davide. Davide
sat back and watched as she skilfully moved Michela's thinking onto happier things. He was very glad she was here. She had a real gift for making everyone feel good about themselves.

It was almost midnight when Michela stifled a yawn and said she needed to go to bed.

Cult of the Dead

Chapter 26
Taking Stock

They chatted informally, as old friends do, until they were sure Michela was settled.

'Quartieri Spagnoli.' Marilyn announced. 'The pillars are at The Monumental Complex of St. Chiara. It used to be one of the most dangerous areas in Naples,' she said. 'Do you know it?'

'Some parts of it, but not well,' Davide told her.

'It used to be called the Spanish Quarter,' she added. 'And guess what?'

'Tell me.'

'It's quite near to the Ovo castle.'

'Are you thinking what I'm thinking?'

'Hypnosis,' she said.

Davide nodded. 'I think the phone call she got the night before was the trigger. They planted the suggestions when they took her to the study.'

'And they brought her back to cover their tracks?'

'Seems likely,' Marilyn agreed. 'The missing phone and purse are way too coincidental.'

'And there was no attempt to take any money from her account.'

'There's something else I wanted to talk through with you,' Davide told her. He set down his notes about the mysterious number. 'More coincidences.' He said.

Davide shared his thoughts on the possible meanings. 'So, it's the four that is the real puzzle. If we can solve that, it might explain more about what is really going on.'

'The verses? Four verses?' Marilyn said.

Marilyn had brought it with her, and David fetched the document from his desk.

They studied the lines again.

'When the Rabbi shelves his tallit, and pacts, at once, with Christ to pray, an exiled Priest be summoned to it, and dark forces muster to evil play.'

'When demons numbered four assemble, over membrane void betwixt the realms, when four servants are taken to resemble, demons rise to gather souls.'

'And darkness draws on power abundant, taking weak and weakened souls, mantle force of good made spent, crossing freely to evil hold.'

'Pestilent curses eternal reign, baked, hot earth scorched to tinder dry, amidst turbulent floods that deign, the lower realms to make the same.'

'The four could be the 'red herring' you suspected.' She suggested. 'Maybe they wanted to throw you off the scent if you got too close to solving it.'

'When I read the second verse, it seems to be saying pretty much what the numbers say.'

'And the first verse?'

'Saul and Sasha. Possibly – but none of us have been exiled, so far as we know. So, it doesn't quite fit.'

Marilyn read aloud. 'When four demons are taken to resemble,' - sounds like it's about demonic possession to me,'

'Verse Three?'

'Sounds like an invasion.'

'Can we trust it?' Davide asked.

'The document is old. Maybe they trust in it?'

'How do we stop it happening?'

'Stop it happening to who?'

They often 'bounced ideas' off one another, using it to ask and questions that sprang to mind as they worked through a puzzle.

Chapter 27
Operation Sharp Cudgel

Cardinal Tolcini weighed up the situation and the options. This was a matter of faith and there was the clear possibility that if the church did get involved it might be interpreted by some as an attempt to curtail religious freedoms. It was a matter that would almost certainly go all the way to the top, for any larger decisions.

Not many of the millions who visit the Vatican each year would ever stop to consider that the Swiss Guards who watched over the Vatican and its interests are so much more than just ceremonial figures.

Each one is sworn to protect His Holiness with his life, if need be, and every one of them completes military training with the Swiss Army, before beginning specialist training for the role.

In the same way that the number of visitors to the Vatican had increased from 1.61 million in 2019 to 6.7 million by 2020, the number of incidents of 'spiritual intrusion,' he knew, had increased exponentially in Rome and in Naples - almost constantly since the covid lockdowns spanning 2020 - 2022. And that was just amongst the Catholic population they knew about.

It did look, very much, as if there was something contributing to the increased levels of spiritual intrusions – certainly enough to warrant a closer look.

That was very much a part of Cardinal Tolcini's own professional remit – but only to a point. The desirable boundaries became blurred when matters showed enough potential to impact on the faith itself. Then it became very much the direct responsibility of His Holiness, the Pope.

He knew that the population of Italy had been hovering at around 60 million since 2020, and if even only the smallest percentage of them were being drawn into occult activity, that could potentially represent a small army.

Historically, he knew, that such activities became even more common in rural areas, where people often saw much but said little. So, if the numbers of spiritual attacks in Rome and Naples were increasing at an alarmingly high rate, as they knew they were, then what was going on at the national level?

Deploying a special detachment of the Swiss Guard in Rome, where the Vatican had its many involvements and was a much-loved part of the social fabric, was one thing. In Naples? Probably not!

If their enquiries were compromised, the press would make a big business out of it – accusing the church of suppressing religious freedoms, or worse. It wouldn't be a good look for the Church, or for his departments.

If an operation was launched to locate and verify the existence and the activities of the 'Cult of the Summonsed,' it would have to be very well contained. They would probably get away with making discrete enquiries and using advanced surveillance techniques to locate them.

They might even get away with some clandestine camera work, but any significant compromise of their activities held enormous risks, in political terms.

Much better, then, if the activities of the cult became known in some more 'innocent' way.

He could risk deploying the Swiss Guard in a 'Locate and Find Mission' using only covert surveillance.

They were very good at it, and if things went wrong, they could claim a legitimate interest in protecting the faithful.

Then he remembered they'd also got Michela de Luca in their care.

He completed the authorisation form clipped to the front of the file, naming it Operation Sharp Cudgel, ticked the box marked 'covert and detached observation only,' and signed it.

Now would be a good time to return Father Ricci's recent call. He picked up the phone and dialled.

Chapter 28
Reconciliations

Sasha and Saul boarded their honeymoon flight to Naples, looking like they were a couple, again.

Sorrento and Amalfi had seemed a pleasing romantic possibility.

Sasha had admitted that she had no recollection of discussing where religion was going to be in their relationship at all, at the wedding reception, and, if she did, she really didn't see or feel any need for any change.

They had made their plans and they would stick to them. She insisted that her faith was important to her and she didn't ever see it not being so.

Saul concluded she must have had a little too much to drink, and he recognised he was no better in that regard.

The flight was mid-morning, and they'd be in Amalfi by the mid-afternoon. He didn't even mind the two-hour transfer time. In fact, they were looking forward to all of it.

It seemed they were themselves, once more.

Father Ricci, on the other hand, was in Naples trying to reconcile the mixed feelings he had about the two main ideas Cardinal Tolcini was telling him over the phone.

Cult of the Dead

The deployment of the Swiss Guard to locate the cult covertly was good news, a great idea, and very much appreciated. On the other hand, the very suggestion that he should ask Michela to make contact with the cult again was repulsive to him on just about every level he could think of.

Michela overheard him telling Cardinal Tolcini that 'it was very unlikely that the cult would even consider another approach from her.'

More importantly, she would already be under suspicion having fled the first meeting, and it might seem 'odd' if she suddenly decided that she did want to join them, after all.'

'Are you sure that's not you being over protective?' Asked Cardinal Tolcini. 'Such things can be explained away if done convincingly.'

'Perhaps. But she's not a trained agent and then there's the matter of the document.'

Michela realised quickly what the conversation was about. She looked alarmed by it, and Davide gestured for her to sit in on the sofa near to his desk, motioning with his free hand.

'What document?' Asked Cardinal Tolcini, pointedly.

Davide had known he'd have to declare it at some point. It might as well be now.

'It's an historical document that we think may be genuine.' He said. 'And it appears to contain some prophesies that may be relevant.'

'I see,' Tolcini said, irritated that it hadn't been made known to him sooner. But now probably wasn't the time to follow that line of discussion.

'It might be better if you come over and see it for yourself.' Davide told him. 'And we can discuss how we proceed,' he offered.

'I see,' Tolcini said again. 'I will...and perhaps you will give some more thought to how we might find an 'in road' to the cult.' He put the phone down.

The last point was clearly intended to suggest that Davide was being too rigid in his thinking about Michela's further involvement.

Davide put the phone back on its cradle.

'I'll do it, Davide.' Michela said, quite unexpectedly.

Davide looked at her, taking on board what she had just said.

He studied her some more. 'Absolutely not.' He said. 'They have people who are trained for such things. It's way too dangerous,' he told her.

'But I'm much stronger now....'

'Absolutely not, Michaela. It's very brave of you, but it really is too dangerous. What if they involve you in the rituals again? You didn't like what you saw the last time, and it could go much, much further. Besides, they'd be suspicious even before you got started, and that really is way too dangerous, for you,' he said.

'I have my faith back, in full,' she began.

He cut her off. 'And then there's the matter of the document. They may still not realise that you have it, which is good for you. What would you do? Just say, Oh! By the way, here's that document I took from you?'

'It doesn't sound like such a bad idea,' she said. 'It would certainly get their attention, and a meeting.'

What she said had merit. He considered it for a moment. They'd almost certainly meet with her to get it back.

His tone changed. 'Michaela, you've been through a lot already, and I have a duty of care for you.'

'Then you'll let me do it.' She said. 'If I do nothing then I stay forever a victim. This way, I consolidate my faith and make good, and I won't be forever looking over my shoulder – whatever happens next.'

He shook his head. 'No. It's too dangerous,' he said.

'Listening is one thing. Hearing is quite another.'

She left the room, leaving Father Ricci pondering over her intended meaning.

Chapter 29
Reflections

In his many reflections over the years, Father Ricci had reached few absolute conclusions.

He thought it likely that in the eternal and complex interplay between dark forces and the forces of light, there could be very few absolutes.

It seemed to be in the order of things, that demonic forces tried to set their own designs and ambitions - whatever the reward that might or might not bring to the individual demon. They could only ever contribute to the overall disruption of good order. Perhaps, then, for a demon, the resultant chaos was *in some not well understood way*, reward enough by itself?

The Church, he felt, provided a model of how things should be. Follow the rules, live a good, considerate life, and avoid the pitfalls were its fundamental practical messages, and all other endeavours by the church sought to support human efforts to do so.

But the complexity of human society often undermined its own position. He'd seen many a good person who fell quickly into poverty and hardship, or worse, purely because society, itself, fell short of the high expectations humans set for it.

Cult of the Dead

Not trying to group people into convenient administrative 'tick boxes' might be a good starting point, he considered.

Often, society fell short at the very first hurdle – the human interface.

Long before ordination was even in his vocabulary, he'd seen and experienced enough of life to recognise that the matter was complex – and then, even before the meddling of any 'dark elements' was included in the deliberation.

Anyway, he knew, beyond doubt, and from his work within the church, that humans were themselves too often prey to the ambitions of the un-G-dly, and they were all too often the most determined and irrational architects of their own undoing – whether by ignorance or by bad intention.

The more he thought about it, the more certain he became that, for demons, adding to the disruption, suffering, upset and chaos of the physical world must hold some manner of reward for the demons themselves – even if the precise nature of the reward remained unclear – when explored from a human perspective.

The eternal battle between good and bad seemed to be a constant wrestling for supremacy between collective good action and collective bad action.

Perhaps when collective bad action greatly outweighed the collective good action, it conferred some greater reward to the forces of darkness, or, equally, to the forces of light, when the balance of good and bad energy was reversed more in their favour.

In the simplest terms he could muster, good action really did make the world a better place, and whatever the mechanism might be that gave the dark forces more advantage when chaos held the greater sum of power, the best way to counter wilful disruption was to embrace the disruption and nullify its disruptive effects.

Marilyn broke his concentration. 'You look troubled?'

'You know me.' He said. 'Always analysing.'

'It has to be your decision,' she announced. 'But is it one you should make alone?'

She'd obviously been in discussion with Michela.

'Whatever you decide,' she said, 'It seems to me that we need a smart objective – one that is realistically attainable in the time we have – and the better prepared she is, the better the chances of success.'

Marilyn made them a cup of coffee, and placed one down in front of him.

'What if Michela opened the door, and we could get somebody better equipped through the same opening? Just a thought!'

She left him thinking along new lines.

Chapter 30
Overlook

Alexander Bolff liked to take the first shift. As the overall commander he liked to check things were right, and from the very start, and if things did happen quickly, he'd be there ready to respond.

Covert ops had a way of going seriously wrong if they were poorly executed, and things often got worse again, if they were poorly conceived or poorly planned.

He checked the view from the window in each direction.

The hired room above the bakery seemed a good choice to begin with. You could see and the street was pedestrianised, meaning that it would be difficult to drive vehicles up at the front to take action against the observation point, if they were compromised.

The manageress was a devout catholic and was happy to help. The rental for the room was a bonus for her, not a need.

They would enter and leave dressed as workmen. The explanation, if anybody asked, was that they were refurbishing the upstairs floor.

He had a slight concern about that as they wouldn't actually be making a lot of noise. Some genuine employees might find that a bit curious

But they could always bring in a couple of extra bodies to bang hammers on a piece of wood, if it became necessary to stay there for longer than a couple of days.

The manageress could always say that there had been some contractual problems should they need to leave any earlier.

At this stage, they were looking for people arriving in noticeable numbers, possibly carrying non-shopping type bags, all heading into or towards the same particular place. There might or might not be some religious regalia worn and partly on show.

The bakery was at work for almost twenty-four hours a day, so arriving and leaving from a later shift shouldn't draw much attention. They could enter through the downstairs shop during opening hours, and at quieter times they'd come in and out from the small car park at the rear.

He checked the camera equipment. Evidence of what they were doing was always important, whatever the reason for the Op was. If they didn't know its full purpose they couldn't be accused of fabrication, later.

He clicked on the radio briefly. 'Mike 4, active. Dark now.'

'Roger, Mike 4. Dark now.'

'Dark now' meant that communication would now only be triggered from the Observation point.

There was nothing worse than a crackling radio in the background just when you were trying to convince an inquisitive third party that you were just there going about your everyday business.

He recorded the *'Dark Now'* on the communications log, and watched from a vantage point back in the shadows, away from the window.

The window here had a low ledge, meaning that he didn't lose much of his visibility by standing off.

He placed a strip of bright tape on the bare floorboards. 'No point in reinventing the wheel,' he thought. New 'watchers' coming in would find it helpful and not stand too close to the window where they might be seen. The tape was a useful tool and marker for when he wasn't there.

There were currently two similar Observation points in other premises overlooking the same street.

He'd check those over during the next couple of shifts.

Chapter 31
Patience

Patience was not a quality Squail possessed. Not even in the smallest of measures.

The frustrations of working with humans and at a distance stretched the demon to its limit of tolerance.

Even the weekly appearances at the cult rituals seemed to have lost something of their initial impact on them. The numbers turning up each week were declining. Perhaps it was time for another Raven supper?

Okil had little to be grateful to Squail for. His withered hand was a permanent feature of his spirit image since the day Squail bit and chewed it mercilessly between its rancid molars.

It had been all Okil could do, not to hit out or push Squail away with his other hand. Had the Marshall done so, it would almost certainly be stood with two withered sets of digits, or perhaps worse.

There had been no option for Okil but to stand there and endure, with one hand squeezing its own tunic behind his back, with all the strength a solitary hand can muster, so that it didn't hit out with its good hand - even when it could feel the substance of its left hand being turned into mush in the beasts' mouth.

He knew it was best to stay silent when Squail was in a foul mood. Patience was not the demon's only absent attribute.

'What say you Marshall? Should I take another supper with them?' Squail turned to face Okil and stretched his face up to look at him. 'What say you, Okil?'

'I'm sure when the moment is upon you, you will know exactly the right thing to do, Demon Squail.'

'Come now, Marshall. You are my advisor. My confidante. Should I eat another?

'Demon, I am but a humble servant. I cannot know the right answer to such things so intuitively as do you, for I have nothing of your ability or experience. Will you take a feast now, and let me give the matter my most careful attention?'

Squail paused. 'Very well, Marshall. Bring them.'

It was amusing to Squail to speculate where the Marshall's meek conversation would squirm away to next, once the feasting was done.

They arrived escorted in by Squail's minions, who shoved them forward roughly.

They shuffled forward slowly, bonded together by the materialised, mental shackles on their wrists and ankles – as the spiritual manifestations of the demon's will.

They were a bedraggled and pitiful sight by any measure. Their spirit was crushed, and their ragged appearances were a direct reflection of the low levels of fight and 'life-zest' yet left in them.

Squail insisted on feeding daily, even when his Marshall had warned him that half the spirit stock would become so depleted they would simply fade away into nothingness.

In the shadows a White *Teufel* stood unseen, and wept silently for the poor souls it had been unable to steer to a better place. It wept for the suffering stood before it and for the last traces of goodness left in them.

Truly, they were damned, for there was so little that the White Spirit could do – not at this moment. Mostly, it wept in anger for their forced cruel existence and their fast-approaching demise.

Okil handed a loose end of the captive's connecting chain to Squail, and took his place at the right-hand side of the demon.

A surge of black energy belted from the demon and swept along the chain, immersing them all in swathes of writhing agony, as it bounced its way backwards and forwards between them, seizing the last morsels of essence in the captives and feeding it back to the monster holding them defenceless.

Most collapsed almost at once, and simply faded away. A few, with more in reserve, fell into a kneeling position and fought on, willing themselves to survive.

One brave soul, bigger, stronger and fresher than the rest, stood proudly throughout, enduring the brunt of the surge as the black energy swept over them, reducing all their energy levels.

Cult of the Dead

Those actions probably preserved many of those who were already close to depletion – for now, at least.

As the black energy began to weaken, Squail put a hand on Okil's shoulder, rewarding the Marshall with a fresh surge of energy to bask in. For a moment, they rode the energy surge side by side, like old friends surfing the inside of a giant wave, together.

The brave soul stood, defiant and strong of will, until the raging force finally subsided and stopped.

'Bring.' Squail ordered.

A minion dragged the courageous spirit forward by the chains, swinging it violently before its master, and then kicked the back of its knees forcing it to kneel.

Squail stepped forward and studied the spirit carefully.

The demon stooped, bringing its own distorted face right in front, reading the strong defiance. A gnarled hand snapped out and seized a shoulder, so that the captive spirit was locked in another long burst of agony. Squail held the spirit until it dropped, exhausted onto the floor.

'That, my Marshall, is how you force obedience and submission.'

Squail patted the Marshall's back. 'You were right. It was good to feast. Did you find me your advice?'

'Demon, from the excellent demonstration you have just given me, I know you will know exactly the right thing to do and precisely when to squeeze the very best out of the moment – whatever the challenges - whatever you decide.'

Squail paused for a moment recognizing the clever use of dark humour, and it liked it.

'Good answer, Marshall. We shall make a demon of you yet.'

The White *Teufel* slipped unseen and silent from the shadows, following the minions to the holding place.

It moved past the minions easily and placed a palm of salvation onto the forehead of the brave soul, filling it with some of its own white energy.

When the captive began to recover, it leaned forward placing a hand on its shoulder.

The Teufel transferred white energy from itself until the soul began to look more clearly defined, and then whispered 'Fortitude' in its ear, before melting away, unseen, still lamenting the extinguished souls.

The next time would be very different, indeed. In that matter, the White Teufel was resolute.

Chapter 32
An Attractive Old Haunt

The hotel was everything, and more, as might be expected from a five star in Amalfi.

The 'Hotel Residence' sat in the centre of the town, just behind the main square, and each room at the front had a balcony with panoramic sea views, overlooking the port.

Everything about the hotel boasted elegance - from the magnificent, wrought-iron staircase that curled up all the way through the centre of the hotel building to its impeccably polished marble floors.

Sasha loved the hotel from the moment they arrived, and Saul was pleased to see her so very excited.

They checked in, and a porter took their bags and led them to their room on the first floor, at the front.

There was an extra surprise when they got there. Francis had been in touch with the hotel and had upgraded their room to a bridal suite. It surpassed all their expectations.

The porter opened the courtesy bottle of Champagne and poured them a glass each while they explored and embraced to superb views, from the double-terraced balcony at the front.

They were not unaccustomed to luxury, but their new surroundings could not fail to delight.

Saul had been to the hotel before, but not to stay. He had no idea, until now, quite how superb the rooms were.

Then, he'd been on a briefer visit exploring the symbolism of the beautifully adorned churches in and around Amalfi Town.

Sasha began unpacking almost right away. She wanted to hang her clothes before they began to crease too much.

Saul leaned forward on the black, wrought iron balcony, enjoying the warmth of the Sun and the town's charm.

That's when he realised that the lady he was absent-mindedly watching as she strolled up to the hotel from the town square, was none other than Annabella.

What were the odds? He wasn't much given to using expletives, but the words 'Oh! Crap,' slipped easily from his mouth.

'Pardon, darling?' Yelled Sasha.

'Nothing. I just spilled my Champagne a bit,' he said.

She went out onto the terrace, with just a gown on, and teased him gently back into the room.

Chapter 33
Lines of Approach

Davide had been expecting Cardinal Tolcini's visit.

He introduced his senior to Michela as they walked through the building together, and then led the way to one of the side rooms set up for consultations.

Davide took the document out from within the folder that he'd left on the desk. 'Here's the document I told you of.'

Cardinal Tolcini studied it thoughtfully. 'It's always good to add to our collective understanding,' he said, deliberately loading the observation with intentional, thinly-veiled, criticism. 'You can tell me more about its meaning and provenance, at some later point,' he said.

Davide squirmed a little inwardly. Cardinal Tolcini was very good at making the strength of his feelings known in deceptively mild ways. He should have told him sooner, he knew.

'You have copies?, Tolcini asked.

'I've sent one over for you in the internal mail,' Davide assured him. 'The parchment has been authenticated to period and the construct of the verses holds good similarity to contemporary documents.'

'I see. So, you believe it may hold substance?' the older man asked.

He didn't doubt Davide's ability or application when it came to such matters. Indeed, he respected it, even when they had their 'differences' from time to time.

He slid the document back over to Father Davide. 'Of course, it ought to be held in the main archive, ultimately,' he said.

He suspected that wouldn't happen but he was not going to make a stand on the issue. He knew the retrieval problems it brought as well as Davide did.

'I have teams in place trying to find the cult centre, as we speak.' He said. 'The commander is a good man and if anybody can find it, he will.'

'That's excellent. Thank you.'

'Have you thought more about how you would like to proceed?'

'I have.' Davide told him that he had reconsidered the point about using Michela in a reintroduction to the cult, but he'd like to restrict her involvement to just the initial contact.

'We can try and use the access to place somebody unknown alongside - preferably somebody more skilled.'

'Who do you have?'

'Ideally, it would be me,' Father Davide told him.

'There's no-one else? Surely your place is here protecting the others?'

Davide knew he was right. He really should be here.

'Marilyn has offered.' He said. 'But I'd want to be sure she was given every protection, and I'd want to know we could extract her immediately if things got out of hand.'

'Have you considered placing a 'quick reaction team' at the observation point?'

Davide was impressed. The older man had nothing of Davide's early life experience but he read every report diligently and had an excellent grasp of the kind of strategies employed on covert operations.

'They'd need to be the very best. Marilyn is too valuable to me to lose,' he said, 'and that really is a good idea. Thank you, Father.'

'Then I think we have a plan.' He said. 'I'll let you know when the observation team has the location, and you can let me know when you are ready to go. If you like, I can arrange for you to meet with the commanders of all the teams so that you have absolute peace of mind.'

Davide was humbled by his consideration, and more than impressed with how Cardinal Tolcini was handling pulling the plan together.

'Father. Thank you, sincerely, for your support.' Davide offered.

'I know we have our differences from time to time, Father' Cardinal Tolcini said. 'But you have my every support in this. You would be a hard man to replace and I value you highly – whatever differences of opinion the work sometimes throws up for us to address.' With that, he nodded to Davide, and left.

Not for the first time, just lately, Father Davide found he had much to think about.

Chapter 34
Anxious Moments

As much as he tried to shut the thought out, Saul found himself being evasive when it came to moving around in the hotel. He was anxious that they'd run into Annabella and he feared having to deal with a big scene in public.

Things were wonderful with Sasha, perhaps better than ever, and he very much wanted to keep it that way.

He knew deep down that he'd done nothing wrong. It had been just a chance meeting with Annabella, and there had been a strong attraction. That was all.

But he was still shaken from the strength of the attraction he'd felt, and even now, he couldn't deny the appeal of those incredible, green eyes

He'd suggested that he and Sasha should go out and explore the town. Maybe they'd find somewhere nice to eat, later on. It would also get them out and reduce the possibility of a chance meeting with Annabella in the hotel.

He left his wallet behind on purpose and announced it to Sasha when they were only halfway along the hallway. "I'll see you at the front of the hotel.' He told Sasha.

Saul went back to the room and had a quick look over the balcony to check Annabella wasn't sat out there somewhere. Then ducked back inside, quickly, to pick up his wallet when he saw Sasha emerging at the front of the hotel, downstairs.

He went down to join her. At least this way he'd have had a chance to warn off Annabella discreetly if he ran into her on his own.

The worry was unnecessary. When he stepped out into the sun, Sasha was sitting at a hotel table talking to a lady. They seemed to be discussing the item of new clothing the lady held up.

Sasha looked as she spotted him, waving past the lady's shoulder.

He was almost at the table when his heart leapt into his mouth. She was talking to Annabella. He steeled himself for what was to come.

'Darling. This is Annabella. She was just showing me this beautiful blouse she's bought.'

Annabella looked up at him, giving nothing away. She held him fixed with those extraordinary eyes, and then offered her hand.

'Hi!' She said. 'It's lovely to meet you. I've been talking to your lovely wife. Goodness! You are a striking couple aren't you? Nice on the inside and out.'

Sasha laughed at Annabella's outrageous comment, and decided that she liked her.

'You'll have to steal me away for a couple of hours, and show me where you found this amazing blouse.'

'It will be an absolute pleasure,' Annabella said. 'We can grab a coffee together, too.'

Sasha hooked her husband's arm with her own. 'See you later,' she smiled.

'Have fun!' Annabella said, waving to Sasha as they left.

Saul was quite stunned. He felt a sudden need to sit down. 'I know,' he said, 'Let's stroll around the harbour first and get a coffee somewhere.'

'Let's go,' Sasha agreed.

The Temptress Annabella finished her drink at the hotel table and watched them walk away. The scent of the residual *Teufel's*, still inside them, dormant since their wedding, made them all the more attractive to her.

But she had very clear ideas about where matters were going, and the demon Squail would just have to 'lump' it.

Chapter 35
To the Devil's Gateway

It was all suddenly very real and very imminent. Cardinal Tolcini had called to say that the team had located the 'centre.'

Davide needed to meet with the commanders.

There'd be a short delay while they closed down and withdrew back to the closest observation point, and readied the extraction team. First, they wanted to place a 'live feed' inside the building, if they could.

Telecom Italia SpA, the telephone company, were very helpful. They put a fault onto the line so that the invitation for someone to go in was coming from within the 'Centre, itself. That way there was nothing to be suspicious about.'

The Swiss Guard agents turned up dressed in full SpA uniform, and arrived driving a loaned Telecom Italia SpA van.

The reach of the Catholic Church in Rome itself is extensive, and it is a Christian duty to do the right thing – even when this involves breaking a rule, or two – and when the intended outcome is a 'lesser evil.'

The telephone company's reach extended to Naples, too.

Cult of the Dead

One 'camera feed' was placed in the entrance way, and the team managed to get another into the main temple room, looking down from the balcony area.

They were almost ready. The focus was now on getting the extraction team ready to go in, should they be needed.

Cardinal Tolcini had also arranged for a police unit to be on standby during the operation, so that power of arrest was there, if needed.

Marilyn seemed totally immune to the arrangements taking place around her.

Father Ricci felt it was his duty as her friend and guardian to see that she was fully aware and properly prepared.

'You have to keep your primary objectives in mind at all times - get in, observe and get out,' he told her. 'Watch always for any signs that they may be suspicious of you. Above all – If in doubt, get out. There's no extra pay for martyr status.'

Marilyn nodded, and smiled at his wry humour.

'I suspect that they have already opened a portal successfully on many occasions. They will be working in and around a Pentagon drawn inside a circle. The Pentagon is a gateway, and the circle is needed to contain and concentrate the energies. But they probably have little idea of just how dangerous opening a portal can be. You never know what will come through it, and once the space contains an entity it may be dangerous to go inside. The circle becomes the boundary. Think of it as a bubble window popping up out of the floor.'

'Can an entity ever step out of the circle?'

'Only the most powerful ones. Most are confined, but a Dark *Teufel* has the ability to do it.'

'*Teufel?*'

'It's a kind of psychopathic entity that has the ability to stay and operate in the physical world we exist in. But it's very rare for a *Teufel* ever to come through a portal. They seem to just 'pop up' in places without needing to be called through a portal.'

He paused giving her time to take the information in.

'You'll have an alarm fitted before you go in. It can be concealed in your clothing. You'll need that always close to hand, and hidden where you'll be able to use it, quickly, should things turn nasty.'

'What happens when I press it?'

'You won't hear anything, but they're very reliable. I insisted on it. The extraction team will arrive as quickly as they can. Probably within a couple of minutes. They'll be armed but probably not firing. They'll take control of the situation, and a couple of them will move forward to get you and physically steer you out while the others maintain control.'

'When should I use it?'

'Whenever you feel the need; if the ritual becomes too invasive to you personally, or if you freeze up and feel like panicking. We only need you to witness and report what you see. You don't need to be personally involved with it. It's better for us that you are not involved unless you really have to do something. That's your call.'

'What's the worst I can expect?'

'If they start to do a ritual that involves you directly. The worst would be some kind of fertility or sacrificial ritual, or conjuring up some terrible demon that starts to throw its weight about. Use the alarm if you see any signs that those things might be about to happen – like if they try to put you onto a makeshift altar - or if any of those things begin to happen, unexpectedly.'

'We can talk some more if anything else comes to mind,' he told her.

He could see by the way that she paled slightly that she was beginning to think about the possible implications to herself.

Good. A little anxiety primed a person for fast action and self-preservation.

Chapter 36
Finding Something Special

It had been decided during Father Ricci's visit to the UK, that Saul should visit the Vatican for a formal interview. It had made sense to combine a brief visit during the honeymoon rather than making a separate journey.

As it turned out, Sasha was absolutely fine about it as it gave her a 'window' to meet with Annabella and go shopping for the day. She was looking forward to it very much.

Saul left early to make his journey to Rome. A hire car had seemed the best option and the Vatican had arranged overnight accommodation.

Sasha met Annabella in the hotel foyer at 10 am.

'You look radiant,' Annabella told her. She was so warm and open. It was infectious.

'Until I stand next to you,' Sasha said, laughing off the compliment.

Annabella hooked into her arm. 'I have a taxi waiting,' she said, steering Sasha out of the door.

Annabella seemed to know all the best stores and what to look at and when to pass.

Cult of the Dead

She took a genuine interest in everything Sasha tried on, telling her what worked and what did not. They discovered that they had lots of similar tastes in clothing.

'Now,' said Annabella. 'We have to get you something very special just for you.'

The conversation became more intimate as they browsed all the options.

Annabella shook her head in mock disapproval. 'We're not having that my darling. I bet you'd look sensational in this,' she said, holding up a sleek and stylish dress.

Sasha hesitated. She'd always stuck to the safe choices for herself. 'Come' Annabella said, 'I will try on the same and we'll compare. Only honest comments allowed.'

'Just let me know when you are ready,' Annabella said, 'stepping into the changing cubicle next to hers.'

Sasha changed and looked at herself in the mirror. She had to admit, she looked pretty good. She was starting to feel quite sexy, and found herself thinking about what Saul's reaction would be. The sleek style of the dress accentuated her figure in the kindest way, and the long side-split up the lower length of the garment provided a subtle glimpse of flesh to just beneath her core. She felt and looked very sensual.

'Ready' shouted Annabella, stepping out of the cubicle into the small changing space alongside. 'Now let me see you.'

Sasha took a breath and stepped out.

The sight of Annabella took her breath away. She looked stunning. The sleek cut of the dress, with its three-quarter length split accentuated her legs, and, as with her own garment - it looked so stylish, and tasteful.

Annabella said nothing at first, and Sasha found herself beginning to have an anxious moment.

'No wait,' Annabella said, as if she knew her thoughts. 'I want to savour every inch of you and to imagine what someone else might see, too.'

She undressed Sasha with her eyes, lingering momentarily where the swellings of her breasts peeped out above her bra, and her eyes slid down past her navel and slipped down and up the entire length of her legs. Sasha felt herself getting unexpectedly aroused.

'Here. Try these' Annabella said slipping off her shoes.

Sasha slipped them on. They were almost the same shoe size too. She saw that her own legs looked incredible, too - accentuated by the heels.

'Now. Let me see.' Annabella took hold of her shoulders and gently turned her around, savouring every curve.

Sasha had never experienced such deliberate, raw appraisal and she found it curiously arousing. It was nakedly unashamed and she could see how Annabella was mentally savouring and appreciating every inch of her.

She'd certainly never had intimate involvement with a woman and had never even considered it. But Annabella seemed so oblivious to her own beauty while completely taken with Sasha's, that she found herself very strongly drawn to her. It was an attraction she'd never experienced before, and she found it excited her.

Annabella turned her all the way around to the front. She felt so alive.

The temptress looked directly into her eyes, down at her chest, down along the length of her legs to her toes, and then back into her eyes.

'G-d!' Sasha thought. 'Those green eyes are adorable.'

Annabella put her hand onto Sasha's hip for a moment, and her gentle, assured touch sent a jolt of powerful sexual stirrings coursing right through Sasha.

'You look good enough to eat,' Annabella said. 'And I find you incredibly attractive too. I think it's time we had coffee. Don't you?'

Annabella squeezed past her and stepped back into the cubicle.

As they changed again, Sasha tried to come to terms with the rush of her feelings. She'd never been attracted to women that she knew of, and although such things were now almost everyday news, it had never occurred to her that she could have feelings like that, or that they could be so readily unlocked.

She was almost changed again, when Annabella pulled open her changing room curtain and reached past her, collecting up all the garments.

Then Annabella took her by the hand and led her to the counter where she paid for Sasha's shopping too, including the two expensive items Sasha had picked out earlier.

It was as if nothing had happened between them. But Sasha was very aware of just how much pleasure and excitement Anabella's brief touch had brought to her.

She felt it again, as Annabella 'cosied in' every now and then, while they walked to the café, arms linked, and chatting.

By the time they got to the café and sat in front of the harbour, she was just about regaining a little composure. Her head was immersed in the power and the moment of her own, heady emotions.

They ordered coffee.

'How did you feel?'

Sasha paused, suddenly not sure how to answer. 'When you tried on the clothing?' Annabella added.

'I felt incredible. Sexy. Desirable,' Sasha confided.

'Let me tell you,' Annabella said, 'I felt exactly the same.

She looked full on into Sasha's eyes and took her hand. Everything I see in this place leaves me bursting with excitement and pleasure.' She said. 'I find myself wanting to be very close to you, as well.'

'How did you know...'

'Your arousal was obvious, as was my own. We women know the signs, do we not? And how can something so natural - so excitingly beautiful be any less 'natural' than these glorious surroundings?' She looked out across the harbour to their front.

'But I am married...'

'It's different between women.' Annabella said. 'Women can embrace the beauty without feeling the need to own it permanently - without feeling the need to possess it. That's the difference between men and women. It's no threat to you.'

'What do you mean?'

'I mean, my darling, that two women can share beautiful moments together and understand that it is just a brief exchange of passion and affection for each other. It doesn't have to lead to any intrusion into your marriage.'

Sasha fell silent, considering the implications.

The pounding of her own heart and the strong rush of her overwhelming desire confused and frightened her a little, but neither could she deny the strength of arousal and the attraction she felt.

'I didn't know I could ever have such feelings.' She confided. 'They were ...are so powerful. I wanted you...do want you. But I have never done anything like this, ever.'

Annabella kissed her hand, gently, smiled silently and then put it down to drink her coffee.

'It is the same for me.' She said. 'I'm not looking to hurt you or your marriage.'

They linked arms, again, when they left the café and strolled by the harbour.

'When is Saul back?' Annabella asked.

'Not until tomorrow.'

'Wonderful,' she said. 'Then, we have each other, until then.'

'Stop!' Annabella said unexpectedly. 'Let me see.' She looked into Sasha's eyes. 'They're turning green.'

'They're not!,'

Annabella took a small hand mirror from her bag. 'Look.' She said, holding up the mirror.

Sasha took the mirror from her to look closer. Her eyes were indeed greener than before.

'How exciting! Just like my own.' Said Annabella.

She took her mirror back and put it in her bag. Then she cupped Sasha's face, gently, in both hands and kissed her, tenderly.

Her breath tasted fresh, minty and vibrant. Sasha melted inside and kissed her back, enjoying the ting and urgency surging through her body.

Her head was spinning with confusion but she couldn't deny the strength of her feelings, and she wanted more.

'Let's go and get a drink, together' said Annabella.

Chapter 37
Placing the Call

They rehearsed the call again. This time Marilyn pretended to answer.

'Hello,' Michela said, speaking into her inactive mobile. 'My name is Michela de Luca,' she said.

'What can I do for you?'

'I came to a meeting last week, but I became ill, and left early. I'd like to visit you again, now that I'm feeling better.'

'I'll need to talk to our president. Can I take your number.'

Michela gave her mobile number.

'I'll get him to call you back.'

'Thank you. Will you tell him I have something I picked up in my confusion, and I'd like to return it, and also that I'd like to visit again?'

They repeated the process with Father Ricci pretending to receive the call.

'You're ready,' he announced.

Marilyn went to the cabinet and took out a piece of paper in a plastic wallet. This is the replica document.

Father Ricci took it from her. 'It's good isn't it?'

'Good enough to pass a visual inspection she said. It's flawless. I've been over it with a magnifying glass to be absolutely sure, and tried it under different lights.'

'Are you ready?' He asked Michela.

'She nodded, confidently.

'Right. You have a break and a coffee while I phone Cardinal Tolcini.'

The actual call went nothing like they'd planned. The person answering didn't seem very interested, at all.

'Are you able to call back later?' He said. 'He'll be in at about 3pm.'

Michaela had kept her nerve saying she had a very important message for the group leader about something that was taken from the centre, and she'd like to return it. She had to ask twice to be sure that he had taken down her number correctly, and she felt she needed to ask him to read it back to her to be sure he'd noted it down.

In the circumstances, it went smoothly enough. It just didn't feel like it had because they had planned for the exchange to go in a particular way.

Father Ricci was confident they'd got the important points into the message. They could probably get away with calling again, should there be a need to.

He went to report back to Cardinal Tolcini that they were now 'operational.'

Marilyn turned up the volume on her mobile and placed it on a wireless charging stand on the table.

Cult of the Dead

They'd leave the door open and rotate duties between them with one person being in the room while the other two rested in the lounge.

The other people in the centre had all been briefed about being absolutely silent if they needed to pass through that part of the building.

Only Michela could answer the phone. So, if she went to the bathroom they'd just let the call ring out.

Chapter 38
Perfect Sunset

Sasha loved Annabella's confidence and kind, funny ways. She had a way of 'sporting' with people but only in a warm and charming way. You could see folk getting a 'lift' from their contact with her, however brief.

They'd both turned their chairs sideways to watch the magnificent sunset over the harbour from the hotel's front seating area.

The thing about being women was that people saw nothing unusual in two good female friends holding hands. It invited no adverse judgement or comment.

A waiter came to the table. 'Can I get you anything else to drink?' He asked.

'Are you closing, then' asked Annabella?

'No Madam, we're not closing. You can stay and drink. It's just the table service out here that finishes at 9pm.'

'Well will you bring us two of your Sunset Boulevard cocktails, and a bottle of good red wine?'

He scribbled the order hastily on his pad and turned to go.

'Each,' she shouted after him.

Cult of the Dead

He turned and smiled. 'What a lovely man.' Said Annabella, loudly enough to be heard by the waiter as he walked away.

They waited until he was out of earshot and burst into giggles.

For Sasha, it was like being on holiday with the best girlfriend she'd ever known.

They drank the cocktails and were most of the way through the first bottle of red when Sasha began to feel a warm, drowsy glow slipping through her body.

'I'm getting drowsy,' she admitted.

'Shall we go up, then? We can take our drinks with us.'

'That's a good idea. Yes.'

They linked arms around the waist and walked through reception together. When they got to Sasha's room, Annabella kissed her tenderly, and then again more firmly.

Sasha looked into her emerald eyes and it felt like she was being drawn into her. The stored arousals of the day swamped her from head to foot, and she kissed Annabella back with an unquenchable desire.

She didn't want their day to end. The strength of her own passion made it all seem suddenly inevitable and gave her the conviction it was absolutely right.

She pulled Annabella to her and into the room and pushed the door closed with her foot.

In the morning, they showered, and took breakfast together.

Annabella was charming, liberating and fun - and so skilled and tender between the covers.

'Remember,' she said. 'Two women, such as we, are a unique and beautiful thing. It brings a connection and understanding you mustn't expect from your man. Embrace it. Accept it. By the way darling, your eyes this morning are the richest green. They're delightful.'

'I want to do it all again,' Sasha blurted out.

They left breakfast half done and went back to the room.

Afterwards, they put on hotel dressing gowns and sat on the large, balcony terrace, drinking coffee, together.

'I didn't know I could feel like this,' said Sasha. 'I don't know if I can stand for it not to happen again, at least once more before we go.'

'It's nice to have a man alongside, too, sometimes' said Annabella. 'When the mood takes. I keep my relationships exclusively monogamous, with just one chosen one - of each. I love the deeper connection it brings, with both. For you I'd consider a threesome – but only if it wouldn't damage us. For now, it's just you.'

She kissed Sasha, again, and began to dress. 'Remember. Nothing happened. Two close friends enjoyed a wonderful time together, is all.'

Chapter 39
The Trigger

The call came back from the cult just after 3 pm. Michela picked up her mobile and answered.

'Michela de Luca, hello.'

'Hello Miss Luca. I'm Titus Barone. I have a message asking me to call you.'

'Hello.' She said. 'Thank you for calling back. I came to visit you last week but I became quite unwell while I was there. Somebody put me on a couch and went to get some water for me. When I came around, I was in a strange room and I was very confused. I decided to leave, but I wanted to leave a note. I found a piece of paper on the desk, but couldn't find anything to write with. It was only when I got home I realised I'd kept hold of the paper, and saw it had writing on it.'

'I see. And how are you now?'

'I'm a little better. Thank you.'

'I didn't mean to take it,' she added. 'I'm anxious to get it back to you.'

'That's very good of you,' he said. 'Why don't you just post it to us?'

'It looks like it might be important, and quite old. I don't want it to get damaged or lost.'

'Actually, that's a good point. Thank you. What do you suggest?'

'I'd like to drop it in person, if that's okay?'

'Of course. You'll be very welcome.'

'And…' She let her voice trail off.'

'Is there something else…?' He prompted.

'I'm a bit embarrassed,' she told him. 'I seem to have left with such a fuss, and actually I'd still like to come and get involved.'

'We have something very special coming up, tomorrow, as it happens. Let me just check. Yes. Tomorrow. Just come as you are. People usually arrive at about 7.30 pm and we start at 8 pm.'

He gave her the details of a convenient place where they could meet.

'Oh! Great,' she said.

'Why don't you meet me at 7 pm? He suggested. We can have a drink and I can tell you a little more about what we do.'

'Lovely. I'll see you there,' she said, trying hard to make it sound like she felt quite charmed by his offer.

She hung up.

Father Ricci ran over and put a finger across her lips, taking the mobile off her.

He found the power button and powered it off.

Too many mistakes had happened before, when people thought they'd finished a call but the line was still open.

'Do you think they believed me?'

'Probably. Well done,' he said, and hugged her. 'Well done.'

Titus Barone looked across his office, to where his minion sat, adjacent.

Cult of the Dead

'She's lying. Never mind, we'll make sure it is a very special and unforgettable night for her.'

Chapter 40
Going Live

They decided not to use a cancellation phone call to bring Marilyn in to play.

It would be better if Marilyn was there in person, especially if she appeared genuinely interested. It would be harder to turn her away if she was there, in person.

They were on their way at 5 pm so that Marilyn could be fitted out with a covert alarm.

At 6.30 pm, they sat in the car a few streets away and began all their checks. They checked they could talk to the observation-post and to the extraction team.

Everything was ahead of the times agreed with Michaela, by telephone, by a full half an hour. This might disrupt any untoward plans that might have already been hatched.

The hidden cable ran down the inside of her right arm and the small, soundless button was placed into her sleeve cuff, where the elastic held it tighter to her wrist. She had only to slip her left hand into her cuff to reach it.

The device was otherwise, not visible.

Marilyn tested her alarm and although she heard nothing in the car, it showed up on the extraction team's computer with the word 'ALARM' flashing on and off continuously on the screen. It

Cult of the Dead

wouldn't deactivate without someone on the Extraction Team entering a deactivation code in a separate computer window.

Father Ricci sat in the back of the car and ran over the main points again. 'Remember; If in doubt -?'

'Get Out,' she answered.

'Are you okay?'

'I'm ready,' she said.

The Extraction Team driver in the front, looked around.

'It's time,' he said. He picked up the radio and said, 'All units, this is Foxtrot 1. Radio check. Over.'

He waited until he had replies from the observation team, the extraction team, and the police team who were sat off waiting about half a mile away.'

'All units, this is Foxtrot 1. Purple Rain. Purple Rain.'

'Three separate answers came back in quick succession. 'Roger, Foxtrot 1. Purple Rain, now. Out.'

Marilyn checked she'd got the replica document in her coat pocket, and stepped out of the car. She crossed the road and began her walk in along the agreed route.

She knew that there would be people watching her all the way in. But she had no idea where they were, and she could see nothing that showed they were there.

It made her feel confident to know that they were so professional. No wonder they called them 'spooks.'

She reached a crossroads and turned right into the street where the observation-post was. She had no idea exactly where.

Her arrival near to the street was announced right away. 'All units, this is Mike 4. Scarlet Trace.'

'This is Foxtrot 1,' said the driver. 'Scarlet Trace, now. Out.'

Cameras clicked frantically in the watch post, as Marilyn entered the building.

'Switch to Live Feed 1' said the commander, and the operators at the computers began to record details of everything that took place in the foyer area.

A man at the desk looked up as Marilyn walked in.

'Hello,' she said. 'I'm here to see Titus Barone.'

The man checked through his papers, and pushed an intercom button.

'Miss De Luca is here.'

'Thank you. I'll be right down.'

Marilyn didn't try to correct the man on the desk.

Titus walked in from the staircase. 'Miss De Luca?' He said, stretching out his hand to greet her.

Cult of the Dead

'Actually. No. I'm not,' taking his hand anyway. 'Michela became really unwell again today. So, she asked me to drop this in for her.'

Titus looked slightly irritated for a moment. 'Marcus, let them know upstairs please – for the numbers.'

'Yes. I will.' He left the desk and scurried away up the stairs.

He recovered his composure quickly. 'Well, it's very good of you, Miss....?'

'Forster,' she said. 'Marilyn Forster.' She gave him her brightest smile.

'I read the document myself. I hope you don't mind? It looks very interesting and Michela was going to phone you to ask if I could visit with her.'

For a moment, Titus looked like he didn't quite know how to respond.

'Well...I had suggested to Miss De Luca that we might go for a drink, first, so that I could explain a little bit more about it...'

'Wonderful. I'll be delighted to,' she said, not giving him chance to back out. 'Lead the way.'

'Er! Right! Of course. I'll get my coat.'

'What the bloody hell is she doing?' said the observation-post commander.

They watched as Marilyn unexpectedly left the building with Titus Barone.

'Camera's,' Alexander ordered to his team members nearest to the window. He snatched up his radio handset.

'All units, this is Mike 4. Scarlet Trace has gone mobile. Copy that Alpha 5. Over.'

The Extraction Team commander nearly dropped his coffee.' He ran around to where his computer operators were, but Marilyn was already off camera.'

'Alpha and Delta! Get out there quick and find them,' he said.

The two operators left quickly and were straight out onto the street, walking quickly. They slowed down as they got near to the Centre so as not to draw attention to themselves.

Further along the street, there were a number of bars on either side. It was anyone's guess which one they'd gone in.

They split up and began checking them, methodically.

Rolf spotted them sitting together in the 'Shaded Tap.'

They weren't wearing microphones so he used his mobile phone, texting the bar name to Heinrich.

Heinrich joined him very quickly, and it looked like they were just two friends meeting for a drink.

They moved towards the end of the bar where they might catch snippets of the conversation.

'I'll just message Susie,' Rolf said. Susie was an improvised name he used for the observation-post.

Cult of the Dead

He typed 'OK – Shaded Tap' in his message app and sent it to the team commander.

'Right! Listen in everyone! They're in a bar called the Shaded Tap. We need people on it, right away.'

They all knew what was needed. If they moved somewhere else, somebody had to be ready to move with them.

Marylyn knew she had precious little time to persuade Titus to let her see the ceremony.

She listened politely while Titus gave her his 'glossy' brochure version of what the cult was about – unique insights, a sense of belonging, a tight knit community and looking out for each other.

She needed to do something, and quickly.

'Are you married, Titus?' She asked, brazenly.

He was surprised. 'Well, yes,' he said.

'Happily?'

'Well...you know, how it is.'

That was a good sign. He was fudging around it.

'Only I have to tell you..' she said, 'This occult stuff is a big turn on for me.' She let her hand brush against his hand. 'Are you in it?'

'Yes,' he said. 'I kind of lead things.'

'Oooh! She cooed. 'I love a man in authority.

'Do you do things on altars?'

'Sometimes,' he said, looking at her to be sure they had the same 'things' in mind.

'I'd love to come and see it.' She looked at his lap, suggestively, and licked her lips to let him know what she had in mind. 'Will you let me see it?' She asked, looking at his lap again.

'If you like,' he said, catching on with the innuendo, and growing in confidence at her sudden interest. If he had to play along with her to take advantage – so be it. They could always deal with it later when she'd revealed her hand.

He looked at his watch. 'We'll have to go,' he said. 'I have to get changed.'

Marilyn downed the rest of her drink, and got up to leave with him.

The team was very relieved when they realised where they were going, and the team commander relaxed again, when she appeared back on the live camera feed from the foyer.

Titus pointed her to a cloakroom to drop her coat. He went upstairs to change.

People began to gather in the foyer, and when the doors opened, Marilyn followed them into the main hall and found a seat near to the front.

'Switch to Live Feed 2,' Alexander said.

The view from the live feed was very good. They spotted Marilyn on the front row and let the Extraction Team know exactly where she was sat should they need to go in to get her.

Two of the cult members pulled their white hoods over their faces and set about lighting candles all the way around the perimeter of the Pentagram. The lights were turned off.

Titus came into the Pentagram from the shadows at the back, and raised both hands.

Cult of the Dead

'Welcome Brothers. Welcome Sisters.'

He broke into a chant, and everyone joined in. 'Om ha bat, Om ha bat, Om ha bat…'

A long line of hooded members processed in and formed up around the circle.

Titus, the ritual leader, or 'Dark Raven,' could be heard above the chant. 'Oh! Great Lord Squail, who hath all dominion over the dark realms, grace us with thy presence that we may serve thee better.'

He turned his back on the main audience and took up a goblet from the simple, stone altar at the back of the Pentagram.

'We drink for thee the essence of the sacrificed, that it may magnify your power and fill us with thy presence.' He held the goblet high over his head, and then took a sip, letting some of it run down from the sides of his mouth. The red wine looked like blood in the dim light.

Then he made his way around the circle, saying 'Drink Sister' or 'Drink Brother.'

He placed the goblet down, and held up a sacrificial dagger.

'Bring me a sacrifice that I may summon the mighty Lord Squail.'

A sheep was led in.

'Oh! Great Lord Squail. We honour you with our sacrifice that you might condescend to join us.'

He signalled with his left hand, and the chanting stopped.

Then he straddled the tethered sheep, briefly, and slit its throat.

Another member took up the goblet and filled it with the blood flowing freely from the sheep's neck, holding the shocked sheep's, fading carcass by the scruff of its fleece at the back, so that the blood could run freely into the open challis.

He dropped the carcass and threw back his hood daubing himself with two lines of blood on each cheek, before offering the goblet around the circle so that the others could do the same.

The goblet was passed back to the audience, who also began to adorn themselves in warm, sheep's blood.

Marilyn watched, hiding her disbelief. Disgusting aspects aside, it was like a bizarre theatre. The operators in the observation point felt repulsed and struggled to keep their eyes to watch the screen.

Titus moved to the centre of the Pentagram, offering his hand as if to help up someone beneath.

Marilyn's opinion changed very quickly, and her mouth dropped open, as the dark entity actually did step up out of the floor.

Squail was in the foulest mood. How dare they keep him waiting! He stepped up into the circle and let go of the Raven's hand. His right-hand grabbed hold of the Raven's tunic and he slung him furiously out of the way.

Cult of the Dead

Titus struggled to keep his balance, lost the battle quickly and slid fast into the hard brick wall to one side with a sickening crunch.

'Kneel minions. Kneel' Squail screamed.
'There is one who is here to deceive me. Deceive me – the mighty Squail!' It yelled.

Marilyn pressed the alarm button in her sleeve. This did not sound good.

The Extraction Team already had their eyes glued in disbelief to Live Feed 2.

They were trying to work out what was causing the large mass of tarnished light that appeared in the centre of their screens, and how it had literally just thrown somebody sideways across the room.

When the word 'ALARM' flashed up on screen the Extraction Team were moving almost straight away.

Police appeared and sealed off the street either side of the centre. Other officers drove in fast, tyres squealing loudly, and closed off the back of the building.

The Extraction Team streamed out from the front of the bakery in two teams. Stun grenades went into the lobby, and then they burst into the main hall yelling for everyone to get down. 'On the floor. Now!'

Squail had disappeared and Titus was still unconscious to the one side of the Pentagram.

Two agents ran forward and grabbed Marilyn by the arms, escorting her backwards towards the doors.

Only when they got to the lobby, did they turn her around to face forward, and then they ran for the vehicle outside, carrying her with them really fast, before bundling her roughly into the armour-plated car waiting with its doors open.

The vehicle sped off immediately and they drove her at a breath-taking speed all the way back to the police station. Only when they got into the safety of the compound did they slow to a more comfortable pace.

Meanwhile, a computer operator in the Extraction Team was urgently trying to get a message out to Father Ricci. She relayed a message through the main ops room. 'For Ricci. Urgent. Attend Bakery now.'

Foxtrot 1 delivered him quickly to the back of the bakery and he rushed inside.

'Where's the Extraction Team room?' He asked.

He bounded up the stairs. 'Father Ricci,' he announced as he walked in.

'You might want to see this, Father,' said the operator from behind her screen.

She pressed play, and then stopped when the smudged light appeared in the centre of the circle. They watched as Titus Barone seemed to fly violently across the room, for no tangible reason.

She stopped the recording. 'I've been hearing that something grotesque 'popped up.' She said. 'So, I'm guessing that's what the smudge of light is in the middle'

She fast forwarded to a point further on. 'That's Scarlet,' she said, pointing out Marilyn on the screen.

'Now watch what happens as the Extraction Team rush in to get her out.' She pressed play again.

As the doors burst open at the back of the room, the entire 'smudge' moved forward out of the circle.

The operator pressed for an extra slow speed, and father Ricci watched with horror as the whole of the 'smudge' moved into Marilyn's body through her back, and stayed there.

Father Ricci went white as the realisation of what he was watching took hold. 'Want to see it again, Father?' Asked the operator.

'No. Thank You.' He looked at the driver from Foxtrot 1. 'I need to get to the police station, fast,' he said.

'Squail was a *Teufel* before becoming a full Demon!' He reasoned aloud.

The operators stared at him, vacantly, not sure what he was talking about.

'Come on, Sir. I'll get you there as quick as I can,' his driver said.

Chapter 41
A Very Warm Welcome

Saul couldn't wait to get back and tell Sasha the news. He had to stop himself from speeding several times.

He dropped the car at the hire shop and took a taxi back to the hotel.

Sasha was awake and in bed when he got to his room.

'Hello darling. How was your trip?' She smiled at him warmly.

'I've been accepted' he told her.

'That's wonderful,' she said. 'Let's celebrate.' Sasha pushed back the sheets giving him a slight glimpse of what she wasn't wearing.

'I've been missing you, in the most horrible way,' she said.

Saul was stunned. Who was this?

Then he noticed her eyes were the deepest green. It must be the light, he reasoned, but he couldn't hide his excitement.

He undressed quickly and climbed into bed beside her. It was like she was possessed. He'd never known her quite so passionate or quite so confident.

They made love several times.

After they'd snoozed for a while, he looked again at her eyes. They were incredible. The only other place he'd seen eyes like that was … 'How was your shopping trip?' He asked, suddenly remembering Annabella.

'It was incredible, darling. Annabella is amazing. I thought about you a lot, too, darling.'

'Oh! Good,' he said. 'Your eyes do look very green in this light!'

'As do yours,' she said.

She took a mirror from the bedside table and passed it to him. She was right! There was definitely a hint of green that he'd never noticed before. It must be the light, he reasoned.

'If it's okay with you, I'd like to go shopping with Annabella again. The day after tomorrow?'

'It's great you are getting on so well,' Saul said. 'Of course. Why should I mind?'

He didn't know what Annabella was up to but thankfully she didn't appear to be out to make any mischief for them, and he was grateful for that.

'She's so funny.' Sasha said. 'The things she comes out with. You never know whether she means it or not.'

'Like what?'

'Well.' Sasha paused, 'We were talking about women's things and she suddenly announced that she is monogamous herself, but she would consider doing a threesome with us.'

Saul looked at her in astonishment, not knowing what shocked him the most – the proposal - or her apparent acceptance of it? Was she indicating an interest?

'Darling, your eyes look even greener! It's such a big turn on, for me.'

Sasha slipped beneath the covers again.

Chapter 42
Hidden Concerns

Father Ricci rounded the corner to the small treatment room not knowing what to expect. Marilyn was in a chair to one side, drinking a cup of tea and holding a biscuit.

'Are you okay? He asked.

'I've seen better theatre.' She smiled at him. 'I won't be dashing back for the sequel. What happens now?' She asked.

'They're all being discreetly recorded as members of the cult.' He said. 'I thought we might at least have a case for slaughter of the sheep, but the High Court in Genoa recently overturned a similar conviction in favour of the right to practice religious freedoms.'

Marilyn looked down, disappointed.

'The church will have a copy of their membership records and will actively pursue the cult with a view to closing it down – whatever is said publicly.'

'That's something then,' she said, brightening.

'There's something else,' he told her. 'There is some talk emerging about something bad happening to their ritual leader during one of the meetings. I think the ongoing investigations are going to keep them tied up for some time. Years, possibly. All in all, I think it is an important 'win'

– even if we cannot stop them from operating completely. It will set them back a long way.'

She thought quietly for a moment. 'What was it? That thing…'

Marilyn looked at him. He couldn't help noticing that her eyes looked quite green. He dismissed the thought quickly. It must just be the light.

'It was a *Teufel* before it became a Demon. That's why it could step outside of the circle.' He told her.

'What happened to it?'

'We're not quite sure yet. It disappeared at some point while the team were going in to get you. But you are okay?' He asked.

'I'm fine, Davide. You know me.'

He smiled, hiding his reservations.

'The driver will be taking us back in about ten minutes,' he said. 'Finish your tea. I'll fetch you.'

He would have to tell her about his concerns, but now wasn't the time.

Chapter 43
Revelations

The two officers in Naples police station could scarce comprehend the information they'd just been given.

'Can you repeat that, please? Slowly.' Said one.

But the woman clammed up and just sat there sobbing with remorse.

I want a priest,' she insisted. Nobody else can help.

After that, the woman just refused to answer any more questions.

The Naples station rang Rome, as it was Cardinal Tolcini's signature that had approved the operation.

The police had noticed the increase in Cult-related crimes too, and the liaison with the Vatican was already proving mutually beneficial.

It was four hours later before he entered the police station. He knew father Davide was busy at the centre in Naples.

The two officers looked relieved to see him and recounted what they thought the woman had just told them.

'It's too horrific to take on board,' one said.

'I think it's better you hear it for yourself,' the other told him. 'Maybe we misunderstood something?'

'Where is she now?' Tolcini asked.

'Back in her cell. We've had a doctor in to check her over. We'll bring her to you.'

They dropped the Cardinal at an interview room and went to fetch the cult member from the cells.

As soon as the door to the interview room opened, the woman launched herself at him and fell to her knees sobbing, with her head on his knee.

The two officers moved to restrain her but Tolcini gestured for them to leave her where she was.

'Father, Forgive me.' She sobbed.

'Come child, surely it cannot be that bad?' He encouraged. 'Officers, am I right to think this woman is not under arrest, just yet?' He asked.

One of the constables nodded.

'Please can we trouble you for some coffee?'

One officer went to oblige him, and the other took up a discreet position standing to one side of the room.

The Cardinal took the woman by her elbows and steered her gently around to a chair on the other side of the table.

He kept hold of her hands saying nothing, letting her sob openly, until the coffee arrived.

'Try to drink something.' he urged, letting her calm herself.

It was several minutes before he spoke. The woman seemed much calmer as she felt the warmth of the coffee pass through her.

'Right my dear. Tell me your name?' Tolcini said.

'Maria. Maria Cantori.' She managed.

'Maria.' He said kindly. 'In your own time, please tell me what you told the officers.'

Tears ran down her face freely as she told him how she'd been to a meeting…a ritual. It was all a bit of a 'buzz' because she was there with friends.

It was almost a dare to go the first time, but this time was different.'

'Go on.' He said.

'It was a fertility rite, they told us.' She began to sob again but regained some control after a moment or two.

'What happened. Just tell me.'

'There was an altar. A slab of stone. This beautiful girl came in from the back, dressed in just a toga type thing.'

'Yes.'

'And then they brought this young man out. I didn't know him, but he was in his twenties.'

'Go on.'

'They made some offerings to the woman, and they called her the Temptress. The Temptress Allegra, and they all bowed down before her.'

'Then what happened?'

'She pulled out a sacrificial dagger from inside her toga and cut herself, twice I think…on the arm.' She pointed to her own forearm to indicate where.

'Then she cut the man's arm, and they spliced their arms together joining their wounds.'

'And…?'

'She pulled him back towards her and lay back of the altar pulling him on top of her.'

'Then what happened?'

'They did it there and then, in front of everybody.'

'Did what?'

'You know. Made love.'

She began to cry again.

'There's something else, isn't there?' He asked gently.

Maria nodded through her tears.

'You didn't know any of this was going to happen, did you?' He suggested.

'After they'd finished,' two of them grabbed his arms and tied him to a cross beam. Not like a religious cross – more like a letter 'X.'

Cardinal Tolcini made the sign of the cross in front of her, and then against his own chest. He suddenly realised what was coming.

He looked at the two officers flanking the room. Their mouths fell open in disbelief and their eyes widened with horror at what Maria told them next.

'The man mustn't have known what was going to happen. He struggled hard and they drugged him with something so he kept still. Then…' Maria's own eyes stretched wide as she recalled her own disbelief at the time. 'Then they stuck tubes in his neck on both sides, and some more into his groin.

The blood flowed out really quickly and they put the other end of the tubes into giant glass storage jars so you could see all the blood filling them.'

'Then they moved the big jars in front of him so he could watch himself die, and we all just watched...'

Maria fell silent and just sat there sobbing relentlessly.

'I think we probably want the doctor back and some sedation.' Tolcini suggested.

He blessed Maria and asked for G-d's forgiveness on her behalf.

When Maria had been sedated and settled, he asked the doctors to examine the two officers. It was no doubt a huge shock for them too.

Then he counselled the two officers in the interview room.

'It's like the Rolls Royce of human sacrifice.' He explained. 'To a Satanist, anyway. It's the blending together of the blasphemy of defiling the altar with the act of procreation, followed by a most horrible form of killing they call a 'leaching.' He explained.

He hoped his explanation would help them to make some kind of sense of the very worst kind of demonic ritual.

As he boarded a train back to Rome, he made a note to ring Detective Sergeant Costa and explain what the symbolism of the two cuts was about.

If his worst fears materialised, he had an offshoot of the Cult of the Summoned practicing in Rome.

The two cuts signified the two sacred channels of 'fertility' and 'ritual human sacrifice' – and it was difficult to imagine two more potent lines of attack of all that humanity considered holy.

They represented a vile form of desecration of a symbolic altar, and a truly evil form of inflicting death on a fellow being.

He could only begin to guess at what reward it fed back to the demon involved, but it was not something that could be tolerated in the holy city of Rome, or anywhere else for that matter.

He felt a tear or two slip from his eyes as he thought about the suffering that young man must have gone through, watching his own life substance flow from his body before he died.

There would be the most unbearable pains as the vital organs in his body began to complain and to shut down.

He knew from his study of the embalming processes that it took about 6.4 minutes to drain 15% of the blood from the human body.

So that poor young man must have watched his own life slip away in front of him in under half an hour, or so.

He doubted very much if Sergeant Costa would ever find the Temptress Allegra.

He rang to tell him the grim news and give more insight into the symbolic cuts left on the forearm.

Cult of the Dead

The police in Rome were looking to see if they could bring a collective manslaughter charge against all the participants, if they could be identified and found.

Of course, the real demons went unpunished.

Chapter 44
Joining the Dots

The matter was far from concluded. Father Davide reflected on the situation. Marilyn was his first and immediate responsibility. She seemed to be okay at the moment but he couldn't shake off his concerns.

The Exorcism Unit in Rome had dealt with any number of cases involving 'Long Term Possession.'

He'd never had to deal with it himself, but by its very nature he suspected a lot of cases would go unreported until matters reached a crisis in some way.

Presumably, the demons 'slept' within the victim and that probably manifested in subtle behaviours that stayed below the radar. He'd do some more research on that.

The operation had been a success in that it would disrupt the ability of the cult to continue – even if they couldn't be stopped altogether.

What it hadn't done, was to move his own enquiries forward in the way that he'd hoped.

It was very clear from the 'quality' of the people involved that they were not the main drivers of any great plot. They lacked the togetherness,

Cult of the Dead

awareness and knowledge that would have required. The cultists were more like 'misguided' victims who had played with fire and got rather badly scorched.

The main architect in this matter was almost undoubtedly the demon who'd taken control of the cult.

That was obviously the intention, or why else did the demon encourage them to summon it, weekly.

Whatever, the reason, that wouldn't be happening any time soon, so at the very least, they must have set the demon's plans back.

There would be a lot of new information coming forward from the police interviews with the cult members. Perhaps that would reveal more, yet.

He looked again at verses two and three on the document.

'When demons numbered four assemble, over membrane void betwixt the realms, when four servants are taken to resemble, demons rise to gather souls.'

'And darkness draws on power abundant, taking weak and weakened souls, mantle force of good made spent, crossing freely to evil hold.'

He underlined the words, *'when four servants are taken to resemble.'* That now seemed to be a very definite reference to demonic possession.

Next he underlined the last two clauses in the third verse; *'mantle force of good made spent, crossing freely to evil hold.'*

He looked up a definition of the word, 'mantle.' It's primary meaning read; 'a beam, stone or arch serving as a lintel to support the masonry above a fireplace.'

It was often a feature of these quasi-religious works that they showed great precision in the words chosen. Hidden meanings could sometimes be found by a careful deliberation of the key words chosen for the texts, themselves..

He wrote down; *'a support for good, holding up the main structure.'*

A fresh line of thought came to him and he checked back to the verses again, realising that he needed the third clause of the second verse too.

Of course! The answer had been there right in front of them all the time.

He wrote; *'over membrane void betwixt the realms,'* A membrane is a barrier and often one that only certain things can pass through.

He wrote; 'over membrane void betwixt the realms,' – *'crossing freely to evil hold,-* '*when four servants are possessed – demons rise to gather souls.*

That's when it all came together in a more certain way. 'When four [servants] are possessed, demons can cross freely between the realms, and gather souls.'

But if Marilyn was but one of those 'servants,' he pondered, who then, were the other three? He hadn't really been able to make any more progress with that crucial question. And it now seemed increasingly urgent he did.

Chapter 45
Facing Up

Father Ricci pressed play and they watched the footage from the operation. He pointed out the strange light aberration that appeared just before Titus Barone was sent sprawling sideways.

Marilyn watched as the Extraction Team entered the hall, yelling for everyone to get down on the ground, and then she saw the sinister looking smudge move out of the circle and disappear inside of her, through her back.

'But I'm absolutely fine,' she protested.

'For now, but what if?'

She thought about it. 'What can be done?' She shrugged her shoulders.

Davide put a case folder in front of her. 'I asked for these to be sent over from Rome.' He said. 'Maybe you should read them? Then we can talk.' He placed a hand on her shoulder, apologetically, and gave her shoulder a gentle squeeze.

Michela came in, carrying coffee, as he left the meeting room.

'What's happened, Marilyn?'

'I'll show you,' she said, pressing 'play' on the laptop.

Davide told Father Gallo.

He'd need him to help keep a watch over Marilyn, anyway, and he knew Marilyn would share the details with Michela. The two ladies had become almost inseparable, as friends.

'I'll show you the footage myself, later,' he said to the other Priest.

He knew he'd probably have to explain what the aberration on the screen was and why it mattered.

Chiara had told him that she'd arranged to go home for a couple of days. She wanted to do her laundry and come back with a change of clothing.

Then he took some time out, alone. He needed to prepare himself for what had to be done, and he needed to quieten the enormous sense of guilt he felt for having put Marilyn in that position.

Chapter 46
Deliberations

His inner deliberations were arduous.

Conducting an exorcism required a certain level of detachment. The Priest's focus had to be absolutely on his own strength of faith, especially when an entity was summoned to the fore.

Then it became a true battle of faith - a locking of minds – and it would be only the firmest of convictions that won through. But how could he maintain that level of focus when it was his dear friend at the centre of it? He acknowledged that he had some doubts.

The select few who engaged with this work seldom spoke of it. But they all knew the risks were high. Heart attacks were a common occurrence.

And then there were the spiritual concerns. He'd known of Priests who had been left mad or completely broken, following an unsuccessful attempt to cast out a demon.

There was the risk of the Priest being occupied by a powerful entity. What then? He turned his mind away from such thoughts. It had to be done.

His mind turned back to who the four 'possessed' might be. He had no way of knowing.

Cult of the Dead

He rejected that line of thought. It was leading into a cul-de-sac of speculation. He could only deal with what he knew to be in the 'here and now.

If that demon was inside her, then it was already a ticking 'time bomb.'

Other cases had shown that there were often significant changes in behaviour in those who were possessed, and that they often just went unreported – which is not the same as unnoticed.

Most likely, that would be the people around the victim being protective of their loved one, and not making any connection with demonic possession. Why would they?

One of the many worrying aspects about it was the high incidence of depression and suicide. He couldn't stand by and watch Marilyn falling apart in that way.

He'd reconciled some of his guilt, recognising that we can all only do our best to choose the right action at the right time. Regardless, of his feelings about it, he concluded the only thing he could do now was to try to put it right.

But was he the right person? That was the thread that plucked, most insistently, at his conscience.

If he failed to draw the demon out, or failed to expel it, what then? It could be years before the demon emerged, and then there were no guarantees about how things would go?

He thought about asking Cardinal Tolcini to do this one, and then rejected the idea, knowing that

Marilyn would insist otherwise, and that she trusted few people in the way she trusted him.

Deliberations over, he went to prepare one of the smaller rooms upstairs. They were all friends. Smaller and cosier, seemed somehow more appropriate.

Chapter 47
Less Can Be More

Davide checked he had everything he needed. He'd asked Father Enzo to be present in the doorway, and Michela would be on a seat placed to one side.

Before he began, he warned them all very sternly that whatever happened and whatever they saw, even if it affected him, they absolutely must not attempt to intervene. 'Please, stay put where you are – no matter what.'

He began to consecrate the ground, blessing it liberally with Holy Water. 'In the name of the Father, the Son and the Holy Spirit,' Amen, he concluded.

He placed a hand on Marilyn's forehead and blessed her, asking for divine protection.

The tension in the room numbed their heads.

Davide began summoning the demon. It was an advantage to know its name, and Davide expected it to emerge more quickly because of it.

'Bah! You dare to summon me Priest! You're a fool,' Squail hissed. And spat.

'Marilyn's head shot bolt upright, her face distorted and pulsing as the demon pushed angrily forward in her body. But it was not Marilyn, right now. He had to remember that.

Davide had learned over the years that it was during the summoning that demons often became arrogant and careless, revealing parts of their plans and intentions in the process.

Most usually, it was best not to engage with them and just move forward to the point of casting out. But a Priest could exchange words, should he so choose.'

Davide chose. 'Your plans have not gone smoothly, Squail,' he said, goading the demon.

'Priest! You are pathetic! You think there is only me? Let me tell you, Priest, we are already four - but I may yet take you in one's stead.'

Davide began the casting out. Entities usually feared this part, whatever bravado they pushed, outwardly.'

'Skallik! Get over here!' It yelled. It's rasping, grating voice seemed even more bizarre coming from Marilyn's mouth.

Michela stood, unexpectedly. Bowed her head and walked brazenly into the circle, joining hands with Squail.

Squail roared with delight at the Priest's astonishment. 'You still doubt me, Priest? I have more to tell…'

Davide was stunned. He hadn't seen that coming, and he felt sudden self-doubt closing in on all sides of his mind.

'Yes, Priest. Now we are indeed two! Now what will you do?…' The demon stood up and roared

Cult of the Dead

with delight. Davide sensed its power and its contempt and felt his position greatly weakened.

'What now, Priest?' It bellowed with laughter. Skallik joined in, laughing raucously.

'Squail is magnificent. Squail is supreme.' Skallik chanted, and both they roared their delight in laughter, taunting the Priest.

Davide began to recite the casting out ritual, holding the cross up at the faces of the demons.

'In the name of the Father, the Son and the Holy Spirit, Get thee Hence, Daemon.'

Squail's mood changed, abruptly.

The crucifix flew sideways as Squail batted it away fearlessly with the back of a hand.

He seized the Priest by the scruff of his collar and raised him up effortlessly so that he hung, suspended face to face, level with the demon's eyes.

'You think yourself better than the mighty Squail!'

Spittle and slabber hit Divide's face alongside the foul stench of its breath.

'Let me tell you how you are not,' it said, 'Your humiliation will be absolute and complete. Then perhaps, then, you will know how puny and insignificant you are to one such as me.'

'I set you two traps by number and verse.' Squail boasted, 'And I watched you struggle to even begin to comprehend my plans. You were so besotted with my little tools of distraction, you completely missed how I was telling you what would happen, and not what might.'

Thorne Hex

Squail spat a foul globule of slime into the Priest's face.

'I spit on you Priest because you are contemptable. You think yourself much better than Squail? And yet, have you not lusted and longed secretly for the affections of the one Skallik now holds captive?

'You think yourself to be cleverer than Squail,' it continued. 'And yet you have not even met my temptress, Annabella, who holds two of your own in her charms.'

'And in all of it, Priest, you failed to see my hidden traps. The etchings of Nostradamus were already there for the plunder. See how I took them and applied them in ways far beyond your meagre comprehension.'

Squail continued. 'Those who were taken - the ones you claimed to be your much-loved friends but whom you failed to protect, Priest, they all fell to the Deadly Sins. 'You let them all fall to pieces in front of your very eyes - in your blind, arrogance and pride.'

'The first one fell to sloth – a spoiled, little rich kid who opened up the pathway for me to get to you by 'toying' with things she did not properly understand - to placate her own self-inflicted boredom.'

'The next fell to greed, for truly he desired my temptress alongside - as much as he desired his newly betrothed bride. He wanted it all.'

'And then that foolish librarian, she took gluttony to be her constant companion, always looking to add more to her attainments, never knowing when she had risked enough. But at least now she has Squail inside her.' It roared with laughter, again.

'But you are my greatest trophy, Priest. How you pride yourself on your ability to solve the mysteries of the unknown. What did you solve? Nothing! Priest. I steered you and your friends into my traps. Now I will take your soul for one of my own, and then come back for them all.'

It spat on the Priest again. 'Bah! But I grow weary of you Priest. You are no equal for one such as I.'

It flung him, fast, and hard, towards the door. His left shoulder blade slammed into the doorframe with a resounding thump, snapping his head back fiercely against the hard wood.

Davide slumped to the floor.

Father Enzo stepped forward to help Davide.

'Skallik!' roared Squail. 'Throw that pithy, nothingness away! To think some might even be forced to listen to the pathetic runt preaching his irrelevant placations…it's too much for a dameon to endure!'

Skallik sallied forward, menacing the terrified Priest, fiercely.

Davide recovered and staggered, still dazed, to his feet, and stepped forward pushing Father Enzo safely to one side, just as Skallig hit Davide instead - at full pelt - and launched him over the balcony.

The White *Teufel* stepped out of the wall, and placed a comforting hand on Enzo's shoulder. It began to recite the casting out ritual, completing the exorcism.

Enzo watched the Teufel work. Perhaps they underwent some sort of divine transformation, Enzo pondered.

'Get Ye Hence, dark Daemons of the void. In the name of the Lord Jesus Christ. In the name of God. By the power and the will of the Holy Spirit, I Command Thee – Begone! Get Ye hence. The hour of your departure is commanded. Begone!'

Skallik and Squail were suddenly gone as if to nothing, and Marilyn and Michela slumped to the floor.

Enzo tended to them, quickly, and then ran and looked timidly over the balcony to see what had become of Father Davide.

The Priest had fallen horribly and the crumpled position of his body betrayed the huge physical damage he'd suffered.

His head lay in a puddle of blood.

The White *Teufel* now supported his head in one hand, and rested its other on his forehead. It looked up at Enzo and seemed somehow melancholy and tearful.

Father Enzo ran down the stairs to help. But by the time he got there, the good *Teufel* was gone.

He phoned for an ambulance.

Chapter 48
Astonished

Davide was sat up in bed when Father Enzo went to see him. His head was still heavily bandaged but Enzo was pleased to see him looking so much better.

'Tell me again, please Enzo, slowly.'

Enzo told him again about the appearance of the entity that had finished off the Exorcism.

'What did it look like?'

'It gave off a glow. A kind of white light surrounded it. And it looked like a Mage.'

'A Mage?'

'Yes. Kindly, Bearded. Wise.'

'And it completed the Exorcism?'

'Yes.'

'What exactly did it say?'

'It invoked the name of the Father, Son and Holy Spirit and commanded them to leave, very firmly?'

'How would it know the words?'

'Maybe it was once a Priest?' Enzo suggested.

Davide thought. 'That's possible, I suppose. Did it look like anybody you've ever known?

Enzo shook his head. 'No. I can't say that it did. But you just got a sense from it that it was kind and well intentioned, and very powerful.'

'Powerful?'

'It had an air of authority about it. You know. Like it knew things. A lot.'

'How did it move?'

'That's the thing. I didn't really see it move at all.'

'But you said it held my head?'

'Oh! Yes! Well, it did move. Definitely. But I didn't see it moving at all. One minute it was upstairs doing the Exorcism, and then it was downstairs looking at you.'

'Did it say anything else?'

'Nothing?'

'You're sure?'

'Absolutely. It looked very sad but in a kind way. Deep compassion I suppose.'

'It sounds like the Holy Spirit personified, doesn't it?'

Enzo thought about that.

'What a good way to put it. Yes. That's exactly what it was like.'

'Have you put all this in your report?'

'Not in quite so much detail. But the facts. Yes.'

'What do you make of it?'

'Well. I ... er...'

'Dear Enzo. Believe me when I tell you that in these matters your opinion counts as much as my own. What do you make of it?'

'Well ...it's all suddenly very inspiring.'

'Inspiring?'

'Yes. What you just said about it being the Holy Spirit in person.'

'Yes. I see what you mean...'

'To think that there might be some entities working with us from within the bowels of hell! Well. It's little short of a miracle.'

'It is rather, isn't it?

'God does indeed work in mysterious ways,' Enzo concluded.

Chapter 49
In the Aftermath

Cardinal Tolcini was a frequent visitor. Michela went nearly every day.

Davide sat up in bed. The bandages had been removed from his head and he was reasonably comfortable. He kept a stick on the bed and he knew he'd never now walk without the help of one. He was lucky to be alive. He knew that much.

'I must tell you about the letter,' Tolcini said.

'The letter?'

'From Saul.'

'Oh! Yes! How is he?'

'I honestly do not know,' said Cardinal Tolcini.

'It's been a most curious business.'

'In what way?'

'Well! His visit to Rome was very well received, and he made a great impression on everyone. The plans were all in place for him to begin his ordination, and they'd even discussed a senior role with him.'

Davide nodded. 'Go on.'

'And then he sent a letter just withdrawing from the process. He apologised, but there was no attempt to explain, at all.'

'That is curious?' Davide agreed. 'He seemed a most promising candidate.'

'Quite.'

'How did the church take it?'

'Well, with every good grace, on the face of it. Behind the scenes they didn't know what to make of it. His father-in-law is still a huge benefactor.'

'Are you sure we can't tempt you back in an advisory capacity?' He asked Davide.

He was suddenly all the more aware of the very real threat to people in Naples now that the Cult of the Dead or whatever they called themselves was there.

'Forget that,' he said, answering his own question. 'You've done your bit.'

'What's in a name?' he pondered, as he made his way back to the office. 'It would certainly make finding what you're looking for a bit easier.' He concluded.

Marilyn had given up her job at the British Library, to take one nearer, in Rome. She was a frequent visitor to see Davide and Michela.

Michela had made her true feelings known at a time they thought Father Davide was very close to death.

He regained consciousness at a moment when she was absolutely distraught at his bedside. Since then, she had helped nurse him back to health almost every day.

It had also been agreed that Davide should retire from the church and move in with Michela – as soon as he was well enough to leave the hospital.

Chiara did what she always did, and ploughed herself into her work. But she couldn't shake the melancholy she felt. It was almost inevitable that she'd be less involved with Michela.

She didn't begrudge her that, or happiness for Michela and Davide. But where did that leave her?

Dropping the work with Michaela in favour of new clients helped, but eventually Chiara decided she'd be better off with a new start.

She sold her business, and after settling her clients in with the new owner, she purchased a one- way ticket to Rome. She'd start again there.

Had she known what lay ahead, she might easily have not boarded the train.

But she did, and two carriages in front of her, about half a dozen cult members were making the same journey. But Chiara didn't know that yet.

Chiara wanted to leave her experience with occult firmly behind. Yet fate had other intentions.

In the dark recesses of the Under-Realms, Squail looked at the diminished movement of the Mantel. Angry, he kicked out with his foot sending the minion who was painting the markings, sprawling.

'Bring that White Teufel to me!'

His minions made a few shifting movements and then did nothing. Confused.

'But that's not possible,' said Olek.

Squail snatched up his good hand and put it to his mouth. Then calmed.

The Marshall was right. He dropped the hand, and began to think about how to catch and hold a 'White Teufel.'

The Church, in its diplomacy, thought it only proper to send out an envoy to visit Saul.

But their messenger didn't get to see him.

When the envoy arrived at the house, there were three cars parked on the drive, and he noticed a real fire was lit in the lounge. But no-one answered the door. He tried for ten minutes to get an answer.

Had he looked up before he left, he might have seen three pairs of dark, green eyes watching him walk back to his waiting taxi.

'Will you miss it?' Sasha asked.

'Not really. Not now.' Said Saul. 'But I did like Father Davide very much.'

Annabella stepped in front of them, naked, and kissed them both, in turn

'What are you thinking, Saul? She chided. 'We'd never find a bed big enough, and anyway, you two are already taken.'

Glossary

Cardinal — A very senior member of the Catholic Church.

Daemon — An alternative spelling of Demon. A powerful, dark overlord of the Under-Realms.

Dark Energy — There is light and dark energy created by the thoughts, words and actions of the entities in the Under-Realms.

Daemons, and other spirits feed on the energy they can take from other spirits or entities. It enables them to cross the Mantles, and also makes their power apparent.

A spirit or soul drained entirely of its energy – is vapourised – no longer existing, not even in spirit form.

Entity	A general term referring to any kind of 'spirit' being or force.
Father	A term used to address a Priest in the Catholic Church. A Catholic Priest is an Ordained minister and has very high place in the Catholic Church, in part because they are believed to take on aspects of Jesus Christ when delivering the Eucharist [Blood and Body of Christ – Wine and Bread, symbolically].
Form	In this account, spirits see each other differently to human experience. The darker and crueller the entity, the more physically twisted it becomes. Like a mirror image of its inner self. Hence they appear to have 3D form when in the Under-Realms.
Gan Eden	The Jewish idea of Heaven. 'Garden of Eden.'
Gait	How something moves or carries itself.

God	In Jewish belief there is but one, all powerful God – as in the Old Testament. Christians believe in a three-part God – father, Son and Holy Spirit, all separate entities but also all 'one.'
Hell	A Christian idea. A place of eternal punishment for sins committed when alive [or when dead, in this account].
Kaballah	A system of Jewish 'magic' or spiritual self-mastery. The famous Allistair Crowley is said to have made use of it, in conjunction with other 'spell books and systems' to create the ritual and magic used by the infamous Cult of the Golden dawn.
Dark Kaballah	The dark version of the esoteric 'Tree of Life' used in meditational practices by some, but in the dark paths, the two sides of the 'tree' are swapped over.
Mantle	Imaginary 'spirit' walls that divide and separate the separate

	regions of the Under-Realms, and restricts movement into the Physical plane.
Marshall	The right-hand 'entity' of a Daemon, sometimes like an apprentice but with authority to act for the Daemon.
Nostradamus	Michelle de Nostradame, or 'Nostradamus.' A seer or visionary who published thousands of lyrical prophesies that many people believe have been shown to contain accuracy about events that have taken place since.
Pentagram	A five-pointed star set within a circle. Often annotated with various magical symbols or writings to create a gateway or portal through which entities or spirits can be invited into the human realm.
	The pentagram itself is neutral. It is the purpose, markings, incantations and intentions of those making use of it that have led to it being associated with Dark Occult practices.

Purgatory	A Christian idea. People who have done wrong but are not yet beyond redemption go to Purgatory – a place of repentance and waiting for forgiveness. From there they will either go to Heaven or Hell.
Squail	The name of the main Dark Daemon in this story. [Imaginary].
Teufel	A German word used to describe a Daemon. In this account there are light and dark, or good and bad 'Teufels.'
	A Dark Teufel is a powerful Daemon, able to move freely across the mantles and enter the physical world we inhabit to inflict chaos and suffering on behalf of the Daemons of the Under-Realms.
	A 'White Teufel' is a powerful spirit for good. Having evaded the temptations and Daemons of the underworld, they become powerful and knowledgeable,

Cult of the Dead

often acting as guides to the newly deceased. They can impart vast knowledge quickly to a newly arrived soul. They become so powerful, eventually, that there is not much the dark Daemons can do about them. After all, even the most powerful Dark daemon must endure some torments while resident in Hell.

Under-Realms   Where the wicked or bad go to, and consisting of the 'Void,' 'Purgatory' and 'Hell.'

Void   The place of arrival for the newly deceased. It is on the fringes of Purgatory and Hell. The daemons of hell try to snatch new souls to add them to their 'Energy Larder' of captive souls.

Thorne Hex

Historical & Author's Note

Burying their beloved twice with the head and the body being placed into separate Ossuary's at the conclusion of the second event reflected the core beliefs of the Cult of the Dead, namely, that the living could 'put a good word in' for the dead, and it wasn't too difficult to appreciate why they thrived and operated only in Naples.

In 1274 the Catholic Church formerly adopted the belief in *Purgatory* – a place for the purification of the dead leading either to redemption and delivery, or leading straight to hell.

Fears that anything less than a full Catholic burial could leave their loved ones stranded permanently in Purgatory probably fuelled the large and early numbers joining the cult.

By 1476, the idea that you could buy Indulgences to reduce or nullify the time spent in Purgatory was also entrenched - so much so that by 1517 it was one of the major injustices against the poor the German priest Martin Luther challenged when he nailed a list of complaints about the Church onto a Cathedral door in Wittgenstein.

The Cult of the Souls in Purgatory (The Cult of the Dead) thrived from 1401 to 1500, and was probably still around in later years when

Cult of the Dead

Nostradamus published his 6,338 prophesies in Italy, having turned his back on medicine and his faith. After Nostradamus lost his wife and his son to plague in 1534 he turned to the occult, and it seemed a possibility, given similarities between the literary features of the ritual and those in the writer's style, the prophesies were a product of those involvements.

Were some or all of the prophesies already in in existence, and could it have been the Cult of the Dead, or an off-shoot derivative cult from it, that offered Nostradamus the way and the means through its occult practices?

The cult would inevitably appeal to a large number of the poorer population in Naples who could not afford Indulgences, almost certainly couldn't read or write, and believed the cult they were joining to be the 'true form' of Catholic Christianity.

The cult emerged again, around 1638 showing that it had not gone away entirely, even then.

Bubonic Plague ripped through Naples from 1656 to 1658 claiming 150,000 dead.

It must have come as a huge shock, in 1969, when the Catholic Church finally declared the cult to be too far removed from mainstream Christian beliefs to be recognised as a part of the Roman Catholic Church.

In such circumstances do people simply desist and fall by the way or do they join something else? Some may continue to worship in familiar ways despite being effectively cast out unless falling numbers compel their reform.

Others may form a new branch of the cult with new designs – for better or worse, perhaps switching to secret meetings to keep their activities better concealed.

Did the Church see or find something else in 1969 compelling it to disassociate with the cult after 568 years of not detaching itself so publicly?

An outbreak of Cholera in 1837, use of the nearby catacombs for piling up the dead in World War II, followed by the Irpinia Earthquake in 1980, most likely helped to keep Naples stocked up with plenty of dead souls to talk to.

The popularity of spiritualism in Europe in much later years suggests a human desire and fascination with speaking to the dead directly.

But if you did find a way to successfully speak with the dead, isn't the next progressive step be to try to bring them back into the world – if only for a brief visitation?

Disclaimer

Please note that there is no intention on the Author's part to suggest that the Cult of the Dead was ever, or is, involved in any kind of occult activity, imagined or real. The existence of the Cult in factual history but only served as a starting point for this story which is entirely fictional.

Any similarity to any persons living or dead is entirely unintended and coincidental – except for the references to Nostradamus who may or may

Cult of the Dead

not have been known to the original cult, and may or may not have been connected in some way.

About the Author

Thorne Hex is a constructed 'writer's name.'

The author has a qualified background in psychology and religion, and writes under the name Thorne Hex purely to add enjoyment through intrigue and interest for the reader - while preserving a measure of privacy.

This story continues with a sequel to be called Sorceress of All Rome. There is continuity through one of the characters in this story.

Each can be read as distinct stories and the author will be delighted if you read both.

Printed in Great Britain
by Amazon